PRAISE FOR ANTTI TUOMAINEN

'Another wonderfully lean slice of European noir by one of its finest exponents. As darkly fun as any Coen brothers' offering' Vaseem Khan

'Hilarious, beautifully penned and startlingly inventive ... *The Burning Stones* cements Tuomainen's position as the king of the humorous crime caper' Abir Mukherjee

'Fresh and witty' Chris Ewan

'Laconic, thrilling and warmly human – hugely enjoyable' Christopher Brookmyre

'A thrilling and hilarious read' Liz Nugent

'Antti turns the heat up with this wryly comic thriller. You'll sweat along with the characters!' Douglas Skelton

'Suspense is uppermost in this adroit mix of psychological thriller, whodunnit and middle-aged rom-com' *Sunday Times* Book of the Month

'Delightfully funny' *Guardian*

'Deftly plotted, poignant and perceptive in its wry reflections on mortality, and very funny' *Irish Times*

'Charming, funny and clever' *Literary Review*

'A delight from start to finish' *Big Issue*

'Original and brilliant story-telling' Helen FitzGerald

'A thriller with black comedy worth of Nabokov' *Telegraph*

'A rollercoaster of intrigue, dark wit, home truths, perfectly gauged suspense and, er, saunas. Highly recommended!' Charles Lambert

'If you are familiar with Antti Tuomainen's writing and dark humour then you will accept that danger never sleeps and may find its way into the most ordinary places, even where you go to chill out' European Literature Network

'Just what you want from Antti Tuomainen, the brilliant moulding of apparent mundanity into a which-way-now thrill ride, with humour drier than a desert snake's belly' Ian Moore

'The funniest writer in Europe' *The Times*

'Another whodunnit, locked-room mystery that toes the line between clever and absurd from the King of Wit, Mr Tuomainen. This eccentric, hyperactive story of murder, corporate betrayal and aging moves at a million miles an hour' B.S. Casey

'You don't expect to laugh when you're reading about terrible crimes, but that's what you'll do when you pick up one of Tuomainen's decidedly quirky thrillers' *New York Times*

'Finland's greatest export' M.J. Arlidge

'A refreshing change from the decidedly gloomier crime fiction for which Scandinavia is known' *Publishers Weekly*

'Right up there with the best' *Times Literary Supplement*

'An intense and darkly funny murder mystery novel' TripFiction

'Weaving domestic life with a murder mystery is done rather well in *The Burning Stones*, with added dark humour' Bookmarks and Stages

'I love how Antti Tuomainen takes such an unassuming, and widely popular, Finnish pastime and uses it as a method of murder – a particularly gruesome one' Jen Med's Book Reviews

'Tuomainen has taken the concept of the whodunnit and stood it on its ear with his signature brand of quirkiness' Loopy Kaz

'Antti Tuomainen is quite simply put, one of a kind in the world of crime fiction. Nobody else could use the off-the-wall scenarios, comedy, and crime and still make it engaging and utterly page-turning' Books 'n' Banter

'Creepy and tense in places, a little comical in others, full of interesting, eccentric characters' Simply Suze Reviews

'Original, hilarious, tense and addictive ... totally brilliant' Emma's Biblio Treasures

'As top notch as always' Cal Turner Reviews

'Nordic noir the Antti Tuomainen way is an absolute joy' Brown Flopsy

'With its razor-sharp characterisation, vivid sense of place and a plot that effortlessly switches between droll humour and compulsive race against time, *The Burning Stones* is Antti Tuomainen at his warm and witty best' Hair Past a Freckle

'Tuomainen's comedy dramas include a hefty body count, but there is something so wholesome and hopeful about them that I'd happily live in the worlds he creates' Café Thinking

'Full of dark humour, intrigue and insightful commentary' A Little Book Problem

'*The Burning Stones* is a beautifully written and engaging murder mystery' Fully Booked

'Quirky and entertaining' B. Robinson

'Antti Tuomainen is a fantastic writer' Portable Magic

The Winter Job

ABOUT THE AUTHOR

Finnish Antti Tuomainen was an award-winning copywriter when he made his literary debut in 2007 as a suspense author. In 2011, Tuomainen's third novel, *The Healer*, was awarded the Clue Award for Best Finnish Crime Novel and was shortlisted for the Glass Key Award. In 2013, the Finnish press crowned Tuomainen the 'King of Helsinki Noir' when *Dark as My Heart* was published. With a piercing and evocative style, Tuomainen was one of the first to challenge the Scandinavian crime-genre formula, and his poignant, dark and hilarious *The Man Who Died* became an international bestseller, shortlisting for the Petrona and Last Laugh Awards. *Palm Beach, Finland* (2018) was an immense success, with *The Times* calling Tuomainen 'the funniest writer in Europe', and *Little Siberia* (2019) was shortlisted for the Capital Crime/Amazon Publishing Readers Awards, the Last Laugh Award and the CWA International Dagger, and won the Petrona Award for Best Scandinavian Crime Novel. It was released as a Netflix film in 2025.

The Rabbit Factor, the first book in a trilogy that includes *The Moose Paradox* and *The Beaver Theory*, is now in production for TV with Amazon Studios, starring Steve Carell. *The Moose Paradox* was a *Literary Review* and *Guardian* Book of the Year and shortlisted for CrimeFest's Last Laugh Award. The trilogy was followed in 2024 by *The Burning Stones*.

Follow Antti on X @antti_tuomainen, or on Facebook: facebook.com/AnttiTuomainen.

ABOUT THE TRANSLATOR

David Hackston is a British translator of Finnish and Swedish literature and drama. Notable recent publications include Kati Hiekkapelto's Anna Fekete series (published by Orenda Books), Katja Kettu's *The Midwife*, Pajtim Statovci's *My Cat Yugoslavia* and its follow-up, *Crossing*, and Maria Peura's *At the Edge of Light*. He has also translated Antti Tuomainen's *The Mine*, *The Man Who Died*, *Palm Beach, Finland*, *Little Siberia,* and *The Rabbit Factor* trilogy for Orenda Books. In 2007 he was awarded the Finnish State Prize for Translation. David is also a professional countertenor and a founding member of the English Vocal Consort of Helsinki. Follow David on X/Twitter @Countertenorist.

The Winter Job

ANTTI TUOMAINEN

Translated from the Finnish by David Hackston

ORENDA
BOOKS

Orenda Books
16 Carson Road
West Dulwich
London SE21 8HU
www.orendabooks.co.uk

First published in the United Kingdom by Orenda Books, 2025
Originally published in Finland as *Tappokeli* by Kustannusosakeyhtiö Otava, 2024
Copyright © Antti Tuomainen, 2024
English language translation copyright © David Hackston, 2025

A catalogue record for this book is available from the British Library.

Hardback ISBN 978-1-916788-82-4
B-Format Paperback 978-1-916788-43-5
eISBN 978-1-916788-83-1

Orenda Books is grateful for the financial support of FILI, who provided a translation grant for this project.

Typeset in Garamond by typesetter.org.uk
Printed and bound by Clays Ltd, Elcograf S.p.A

For sales and distribution, please contact *info@orendabooks.co.uk*

HELSINKI, 1982

1

He wanted to see it one last time before he left.

Ilmari Nieminen looked at the piano, its shiny black exterior and ivory-white keys, like an almost endless row of bright, Hollywood teeth. The pedals looked clean, like freshly polished cutlery; its sides gleamed like ice in the moonlight.

His daughter's piano.

In six days' time.

As long as they could agree on one important thing.

Ilmari turned, looked around for an assistant and, as he did so, glanced outside.

Beyond the windows, underlined by the dark-green store logo, were the Christmas lights of Aleksanterinkatu, sparkling in gold and yellow. Large snowflakes, the size of wood shavings, slowly fell from the sky, gently rocking from side to side. The difference between the outdoor and indoor temperatures must have been around forty degrees. In the clammy warmth of the instrument store, one Christmas carol ended and another began, and before long the snow once more lay round about, deep and crisp and even.

'Looking for a piano?'

Ilmari turned again and couldn't tell where the exceptionally tall salesman in the polka-dot shirt had appeared from. He must have been lurking nearby, behind another piano, perhaps. Which seemed tricky, not least because of his height. Still, Ilmari didn't want to think about the matter any further. He didn't have time.

'Yes, as a matter of fact,' he replied, and pointed at the piano. 'This one. I want to make sure this piano will still be here in six days' time.'

The salesman looked at the piano, then at Ilmari. He seemed hesitant.

'That's Christmas Eve,' he said.

'That's why I'm asking,' said Ilmari.

The salesman nodded, still hesitant. 'A piano for Christmas, then,' he said.

Ilmari confirmed this was precisely the case, and he was about to get to the main point but was cut short.

'You'll have to order the delivery today,' said the salesman. 'At the latest.'

'That won't be necessary,' said Ilmari. 'All I need is for this piano to be here on Christmas Eve. I'll deliver it myself.'

The salesman said nothing. The tiny, plum-blue dots on his shirt seemed to shimmer against their black background. Ilmari tried not to look at the restless shirt and attempted instead to form an overall picture of the man. He was extremely tall and extremely thin. Ilmari couldn't dispel the image of him folding and unfolding himself behind the pianos, waiting for a customer to appear.

'So, if I've understood right,' the salesman began, and Ilmari saw a cautious smile burgeoning on his long, patient face, 'you'd like to buy the piano now and collect it on Christmas Eve. In that case, I'd be more than happy to sell it to you. An excellent choice, I must say; I have the same model at home. And this is the last one we have.'

His last sentence didn't sound like a sales pitch. In fact, nothing he said sounded like a sales pitch.

'The last one?' Ilmari asked.

'We won't be getting any more this year,' he replied, sounding as though he was genuinely upset and not merely trying to push the sale. 'This is the only one.'

They both looked at the piano and, probably because of this new information, something in Ilmari now saw it for the first time.

Though, of course this wasn't the first time.

The first time had been almost two months ago, when Helena, his twelve-year-old daughter, had brought him into the store and shown him what she wanted for Christmas; now that she had started piano lessons with a renowned teacher and had made such swift progress, she'd decided she wanted to become a concert pianist. She had sat down at this piano and started playing, and Ilmari had known he couldn't tell her about his money problems, or about the fact that since the divorce, with Helena and her mother keeping the apartment, the lion's share of Ilmari's wage from the postal sorting office was spent on the mortgage, child-support payments and his own rent, and that right now the only things in his wallet were his driving licence and his yearly ticket to the Film Archive. Ilmari hadn't breathed a word about any of this. Instead, he had tried to hide how moved he was to see Helena's fingers dancing across the keys and, above all, to listen to what her fingers and the keys produced together. And as Helena had finished playing and stood next to the piano, that's when Ilmari had made his decision.

He had promised her that piano, and he'd promised it for Christmas.

And now, six days before Christmas Eve, he was standing on the first floor of that same music store with a nervous salesman a full head taller than him, trying to find a solution to a problem that had taken on new dimensions. At the same time, still looking at the salesman's rapidly blinking eyes, he started to sense something else too. He found himself thinking that he and the salesman might have something in common after all.

'I don't remember you from last time,' said Ilmari.

'Pardon me?'

'I visited the store two months ago.'

'I didn't work here then,' the man said with a shake of the head. 'In fact, I only started five days ago.'

Ilmari waited, sensing that the salesman wasn't finished.

'I'm a composer,' he said eventually. 'But composing doesn't ... And, seeing as I know these instruments quite well, I thought ... Work and pleasure, you know ... But this job is mostly commission-based, and I ... as I said, I'm a composer, and I suppose I don't really...'

'I understand,' said Ilmari. 'I'm in a similar situation myself.'

'You're a composer too?'

'I'm a postman,' he said. 'And I'm buying a piano. But I won't have the money until Christmas Eve, and I'd like to reserve this piano now. Especially as it's the last one.'

The salesman looked at Ilmari, and Ilmari thought he now appeared even more pained than before.

'But, without the money, without any downpayment, I don't think I can ... I'm not sure my boss will allow...'

'I suggest a slightly unusual arrangement,' Ilmari began. 'I will reserve the piano now, and when I collect it on Christmas Eve, I will pay the full manufacturer's suggested retail price, meaning you will get the maximum commission. On top of this, I'll pay, let's say, ten percent extra as a reservation and storage fee – or whatever you want to call it. You can enter it in the books however you please.'

The salesman swallowed. Ilmari could see that the composer knew how to count.

'That would save Christmas,' said the composer.

'That would save Christmas,' Ilmari agreed.

The composer looked first at the piano, then at Ilmari.

'If I reserve this piano for you, how do I know that you really will come back on Christmas Eve?'

'Because I've given you my word,' said Ilmari. 'Because this is my daughter's piano.'

2

Ilmari walked through the blizzard to Kamppi, found the right bus stop, waited fifteen minutes in the freezing cold, then climbed on board the number thirty-nine bus, dipped his ten-ticket travel card – now a little softened from sitting in his pocket – into the machine and allowed it to punch the final hole in the corner. He took a seat by the window near the back of the bus and felt warm air from the heater blowing against his left shin. The bus filled up one stop at a time and started to smell of damp clothes, as the snow melted on people's jackets, shoes and woolly hats. He got off the bus in Pitäjänmäki. The snow had gathered in trenches along the pavements of this industrial neighbourhood, so Ilmari had to fight his way through it. According to the map that he had torn out of the telephone directory, his destination was around one kilometre from the bus stop.

Ilmari trudged through the snow, thinking to himself.

When the offer had presented itself, he had leapt at it. Despite the fact that he didn't even know the guy. He'd got the tip-off and the phone number from Riekkonen, one of his older colleagues at the sorting office. At the end of the day, he was very low on options. He couldn't ask his parents for money for the simple reason that they never had any, except to spend on cigarettes and alcohol; they were barely able to look after themselves. And as for friends from his youth and early adulthood, they had all practically disappeared after starting families of their own. And in any case, it was unlikely they would have been able to lend an old school mate enough money to buy a piano. All in all, this job offer and the payment he would get

would solve his problem. And this was why he had decided to
take four days' unpaid leave from his proper job at the post office,
and why, as evening drew in, he now found himself walking
towards an industrial area in northern Helsinki, only days before
Christmas, his final destination: Kilpisjärvi – right at the other
end of the country.

He passed various warehouses and factory buildings, most of
which were unlit. It was as though the streetlamps were
positioned further apart than they were downtown; the dark
blind spots between the lights appeared to be getting longer.
Ilmari tugged his mittens up his wrists, as the wind seemed to be
targeting them with particular accuracy. Snowflakes tingled on
his face, where they melted and dripped down inside his collar.

Finest Antiques & Furniture, read a faint blue-and-white neon
sign, its lower edge slightly hanging off the wall. He had arrived.
At first, Ilmari thought this was yet another unilluminated, two-
storey, roughcast construction, until he noticed a light at the
other end of the building. He walked to the window, and
through the Venetian blinds he saw slices of a poster of Victoria
Principal and a cluttered desk on which sat several calculators.
He located the bell in the doorway, and before its sound had
faded, the door opened, and the frozen air was mixed with a
curious blend of aftershave and onion. Ilmari had barely
introduced himself and explained why he was here when the man
showed him inside.

'Pentti Leinonen,' said the man. 'The finest antiques.'

Ilmari brushed the snow from his jacket and scarf, pulled the
hat from his head and followed Leinonen further into the
building. They went through another door into the furniture
showroom. Leinonen switched on the lights, and Ilmari looked
around. He saw an array of items, mostly furniture of various
ages, though none of it was exactly antique, let alone of the finest

quality. Some of the items were nothing more than junk: heaps of lamps, piles of rugs, stacks of paintings. He looked at the middle-aged man next to him, who smelt of Tabac and meat pasty, and only now did he notice that the man's right eye was made of glass and stared in a slightly different direction to his left.

'Need any furniture?' Leinonen asked.

'No, thank you,' Ilmari replied.

For a moment, they stood in silence. Leinonen wasn't the person Ilmari had spoken with on the phone, and he felt a level of relief at the thought.

'The prices are all tax-free,' said Leinonen.

'I came to pick up the car,' said Ilmari.

They stood on the spot a moment longer, then Leinonen walked off, and Ilmari followed him once again, which was obligatory as corridors the width of woodland pathways were the only routes through the clusters of junk. But what set this place apart from the woods was its smell: the odour of mould was thick and sour. Leinonen stopped, and Ilmari saw that they had reached the gable facing the road, where there was a roll-up door. And in front of the roll-up door was a van. If you could call it that.

'I understood from our phone call,' Ilmari began, 'that you'd been asked to find a second-hand Fiat Ducato, or something similar.'

'After expenses and deductions,' said Leinonen, 'and given the timeframe, completely out of the question. This one would have been out of the question too, if I hadn't chipped in a bit of my own.'

Now Ilmari realised what it was about Leinonen that disturbed him. It wasn't the combined aroma of meat and rice and perfume committing a full-frontal assault on Ilmari's senses, or Leinonen's eyes, with which it was impossible to make any kind of contact. It was the way he seemed to approach everything: he might not have been entirely dishonest, but this was the kind of guy you wouldn't want to buy a second-hand car from. During their short acquaintance, Leinonen had told him he offered the finest antiques while surrounded by piles of junk, suggested a spot of tax avoidance, and now it seemed he was hiding some of the money used to acquire the van. In one instance, however, Leinonen had told the truth, and in that he was perhaps more correct than he knew.

There was no time for anything else.

The light-blue van was a Thames, a British vehicle. Ilmari wasn't an expert, but he was relatively certain this particular model had been discontinued some time ago.

'I put on some winter tyres for you,' said Leinonen.

Ilmari walked around the van, checked the undercarriage and the tyres, and saw that the latter were newish, but that there was one type on one side of the van and a different type on the other, which meant they were more than likely stolen and, what's more, from two different vehicles. Ilmari arrived at the back door, opened it and concluded that, in this respect, everything was as it should be.

That said, seeing the sofa in the back of the van was like stumbling upon the Koh-I-Noor diamond in a sweaty changing room.

Unlike everything else Ilmari had seen in this cluttered warehouse, the generous sofa squished into the back of the van really was the finest of antiques. The dark-red upholstery was opulent, the dark-brown wooden fixtures gleamed. Ilmari could easily understand how this skilfully restored sofa might be important to someone, and not only in terms of its monetary value, though naturally that must play a part. He looked at the sofa a moment longer, checked the fastenings and tightened the straps on both sides, and closed the door. Then he walked round to the driver's side and opened the door. The keys were in the lock, the tape player looked new and everything else looked old. The driver's seat looked as though a very heavy driver had been sitting in it for several decades. Which, of course, was entirely possible.

'As you can see, this vehicle is specifically for long-haul journeys,' said Leinonen. 'I took that into account – when I heard you weren't taking the most direct route.'

'I'm going to stop in Ilomantsi on the way,' said Ilmari, more to himself than to Leinonen. 'Then Vaasa.'

'I know a lot of people in both towns,' said Leinonen. 'Smashing places.'

Ilmari thought it all but certain that Leinonen had never visited either town. Without continuing the conversation, he walked around the vehicle one more time, opened the passenger door and checked the dashboard on that side. He inspected the old van's interior for a while then took a deep breath. Very well, he thought. He would drive the van and the sofa all the way north to Kilpisjärvi, so he could buy his daughter a piano for Christmas. Everything else was of secondary importance. What did it matter if he froze, how uncomfortable the seat was or how difficult it was to drive an old English van in the harsh Finnish winter?

'Did you bring the money?' asked Leinonen once Ilmari had closed the door.

Ilmari walked up to him. 'What money?'

'Seeing as you're renting the car,' Leinonen added, both his eyes now avoiding direct contact.

Ilmari had only known Leinonen a matter of minutes, but he could already say that he was a man who would never stop trying his luck. The mere whiff of cash would make him try and pull a fast one.

'That isn't the arrangement, and you know it,' said Ilmari. '*You're* supposed to give *me* money – for the petrol.'

He said nothing further. He stood in front of Leinonen long enough that beads of sweat began pushing their way out of Leinonen's forehead as he clenched his thumbs in his fists. Eventually, Ilmari managed to make contact with Leinonen's working eye. He heard Leinonen swallow.

'I remembered wrong,' said Leinonen. 'When you do a lot of business, you forget the details.'

From his back pocket, he took a glossy brown envelope. Ilmari took it, opened it and counted the money. The sum was just enough to cover the petrol, but nothing else. Ilmari slid the envelope into his jacket pocket.

'Will you open the door?' he asked Leinonen and sat in the car.

'The map's in the glove compartment,' Leinonen called as he strode towards the roll-up door and flicked a switch.

The door rose with a squeal. The snowflakes floating outside sensed it was opening and rushed in. Once the door was fully open, Ilmari started the engine and managed to put the van in gear on the second attempt. Then he carefully steered the English classic out into the frozen weather and towards the gate and the street beyond it, and, without looking back, headed east to Ilomantsi.

At least, this was his intention.

As he accelerated out of the junction and onto the Ring Road around the city, he noticed he was driving without functioning windscreen wipers. Normally, or in any normal vehicle, this wouldn't necessarily be a problem: you don't usually need windscreen wipers in the dead of winter. But the Thames wasn't a normal vehicle in this sense, or in any sense. The way in which the barrel-shaped heater in the footwell pumped hot air into the cab meant that the almost vertical windscreen above it heated up and seemed to attract the billowing snowflakes like a magnet before only partially melting them. Before he'd even reached the next junction, Ilmari knew he had a problem.

As he drove, he wound down the side window, leant forwards, reached a hand out of the cab and wiped the windscreen from the outside with his mitten. Just then, he saw the lights of a Teboil petrol station up ahead. He took the slip road off the dual carriageway, pulled into the forecourt of the petrol station and parked in a row of vehicles outside the repair garage. He sat in the cab for a moment and thought through his options, before quickly concluding that he had very few. He hoped he was wrong. He pulled on his woolly hat, stepped out of the van, locked the door, walked to the garage and learnt that he had been right after all.

There were no spare parts for the Thames, and the next time anyone could have at least assessed the situation would be late afternoon the following day.

The assistant, with a head of bright, peroxide-startled hair, nonetheless tried to be as friendly as she could, clearly wanting to show empathy in the face of Ilmari's misfortune. The garage smelt of oil and grease, and from the loudspeakers in the cafeteria Ilmari heard how many partridges had once sat in a pear tree.

'Where are you heading?' the woman asked.

'Up north,' said Ilmari, then added, 'eventually.'

'Dear, oh dear,' she said. 'Then we need to get those blades working. You'd need to be Ari Vatanen just to keep that thing on the road.'

Ilmari thought even the newly crowned rally world champion himself would think twice before driving the Thames – assuming the Thames ever got back on the road. Ilmari couldn't think of anything else to say – maybe there wasn't anything to say – so he thanked the woman for her help and turned towards the door.

'I hope you get the wipers working again,' she called after him. 'It's going to be murder up north.'

Her last sentence rang in Ilmari's ears. It was more a curse than a weather forecast, and felt ominous, not least because he was missing both parts and a mechanic.

He walked across the brightly lit forecourt towards the van, avoiding the slippery furrows smoothed by hundreds of tyres, and trying to think which service station he could stop at next, because there was only one thing that mattered: he had to get going.

Lost in thought as he stepped across another patch of ice, he heard a voice behind him.

'My old man used to have a Thames,' someone said. 'Ask inside for a set of pliers and a Phillips screwdriver, and I'll fix your wipers.'

3

Pitäjänmäki was like a massive fanny: dark, slippery and a mystery to mankind. Otto Puolanka gripped the steering wheel and drove past the building twice before realising it was the one he was looking for. *Finest Antiques & Furniture.* He steered the car through the gate and pulled up by the wall, switched off the engine of his old Saab 96, stumped his Camel into the already full ashtray, managing to spill ash on the passenger seat, then stuck his right hand into the footwell at the back and groped around for his drink. Eventually, he located the half-full bottle of cheap vodka and unscrewed the lid. As he raised the bottle to his lips, he saw tyre tracks in the snow. If he hadn't been used to drinking straight from the bottle, he would have spat the liquor into his lap. He was already furious, but now he could feel waves of anger heaving within him, a storm rising.

The tracks started from the roll-up door, curved towards the gate, mixed with other tracks, then disappeared altogether.

This meant he was late.

Otto didn't know why, every time he popped into the bar to perk himself up, he ended up staying longer than he'd planned. He had simply intended to rinse the stale taste of vodka from his mouth with some cool, crisp lager, and he'd calculated that he had plenty of time to do this – but before he knew it, he'd ended up playing darts and having not one but three pints.

He screwed the lid back in place. He needed a refill.

He opened the door and stepped out into the cold. The wind was stronger now, the snow attacked his eyes and ears. Otto took a pack of Camels from his right pocket, lit a fresh cigarette and trudged through the snow to the door, mentally cursing all the way. His knee-length leather jacket kept out the wind, but because he didn't have any gloves, his fingers felt the chill. He rang the buzzer, exhaling smoke into the winter's evening.

The door opened, and Otto stepped inside.

'Pentti Leinonen,' said the pungent-smelling man who opened the door. 'The finest antiques.'

Otto said nothing. He took the man by the arm, gripped him tightly and walked him into the furniture warehouse. Once inside, Otto released his grip and took the cigarette from his lips with a cupped hand.

'No smoking in here,' said the man who had introduced himself as Leinonen. 'You wouldn't do that in Sotheby's.'

'Where's the sofa?' asked Otto.

'What sofa?'

Otto wanted to look the man in the eyes, but he couldn't find them. Well, of course he knew that the eyes are generally located in a person's head, approximately in the middle, but for some reason making contact with these particular eyes seemed all but impossible. Otto defiantly filled his lungs with smoke again, then exhaled and looked around. He felt drunk, but more than that, he was furious. It was often hard to tell the two apart.

'You know what sofa,' he said. 'And another thing. I saw tyre tracks in the snow. What kind of car is it?'

'What's this all about?' asked Leinonen. 'We only sell antiques of the highest quality—'

'This is a low-life hiding place for stolen goods,' Otto retorted. 'So I'll ask you again: where is the sofa and what make is the car?'

Leinonen's tongue ran across his lips, as though greasing them for use. Then he stood up straighter – or tried to, at least.

'How much?' he said. 'If I might ask, between friends. How much are you willing to pay for that kind of information?'

'Between friends?'

'Yeah.'

'Pay?'

'Yeah...' Leinonen hesitated. He looked confused.

Otto dropped his cigarette on the floor but did not stamp it out. Leinonen again ran his tongue across his lips, but this time he didn't say anything.

'Don't friends usually help one another?' asked Otto. 'For free? Without payment? You really want us to be friends?'

'You what?'

'Would you answer my personal ad?' asked Otto. '"Looking for a friend. Photo replies only."'

'What?'

'"I'm into music,"' Otto continued. '"You don't have to dig the same music as me, as long as you're a nice guy."'

'What?'

Otto clenched his fists, opened and closed them. His joints cracked.

'"P.S.,"' he continued. '"Layabouts, don't bother."'

'You're crazy,' said Leinonen.

Otto took a deep breath. Sooner or later, everybody said the same thing. You couldn't trust people; he'd learnt that. That's why he didn't have friends, and that's why he couldn't find friends. And why had he dropped his cigarette on the floor? He needed a cigarette. He shoved his hand into his left pocket – and yelled. The pain was dizzying, excruciating. He pulled his hand out of his pocket, looked at where he'd stuck his finger, what had jammed its way under the nail of his forefinger.

The darts.

He understood what had happened. The vodka. The thirst. The bar. The lager. The darts. Which had ended up in his pocket.

A second later, he realised something else too.

The man calling himself Leinonen was trying to run past him.

Otto quickly raised his hand. His sole intention was to stop him, but the man's surprisingly powerful lunge, the strength of Otto's flick of the hand, and the pack of darts he was gripping in his fist combined forces, and all five darts sank into the man's cheek like needles into a pin cushion.

Leinonen stopped, looking both as though he had realised something important and run headlong into a wall. Otto was still holding on to the darts. He released his grip and stared at the man in front of him, who now had a full set of red-flighted darts in his right cheek and was shifting his weight from one leg to the other, his hands flailing through the air.

'Ay em ou,' the man called Leinonen said – or shouted, more like.

At first, Otto didn't understand what the man was saying, but then he thought he knew. 'Take them out,' he was saying, over and over again. Otto walked up to the man, gripped the darts with one hand and the man's head with the other, then ripped the darts out of his cheek. Blood sprayed like a tin of paint punctured with a fork. The man called Leinonen slapped himself on the cheek, held his hand there and looked like he was finally ready to talk.

'The sofa's in a van on its way to Ilomantsi, then Vaasa, and finally to Kilpisjärvi,' he said eventually. 'It's an old, light-blue Thames, a British van. A quality motor.'

For a moment, Otto considered what he had just heard. He looked at the man with blood dripping between his fingers and onto the floor and bubbling at the corner of his mouth.

'I'd expected something newer,' said Otto. 'A Fiat Ducato or something similar.'

Now, on top of everything else, the man called Leinonen was getting agitated.

'Everybody's complaining about that bloody van,' he said. 'It was the best I could get in the timeframe—'

'By everybody,' Otto began, 'I suppose you mean the driver? What does he look like?'

'What does he ... look like?'

Otto was starting to run out of what patience he had left.

The man appeared to sense this. 'Shorter than you,' he said quickly. 'Slimmer than you, long, dark hair, a bit of a rocker, brown eyes, a high collar on his jacket ... That's all I can remember. But despite his build, somehow ... threatening or ... determined or...'

'Threatening?' said Otto. 'Or determined?'

'Well,' the man called Leinonen began. 'He knows what he wants. And he won't stop until he gets it. That's the impression I got. He's somehow ... uncontrollable ... unstoppable even.'

Otto spat on the floor, as though he had again tasted something rancid that didn't belong in his mouth. The man called Leinonen looked at him.

'Believe you me, nobody's unstoppable,' said Otto. 'When did he leave?'

The man looked to the side. Otto followed his eyes and was taken aback. The grandfather clock showed the right time.

'Half an hour ago,' said Leinonen.

If the man and the sofa were on their way to Ilomantsi, they would head east out of the city and drive towards Porvoo, then turn onto Highway 6 before Loviisa. If Otto squeezed everything he could out of the Saab, he might catch up with the old van before Kouvola and would be back in Helsinki by morning. He had been hired to deliver the sofa to a client – it didn't matter to him who it was – and that is what he intended to do. That was how he operated, and his reputation depended on it. He got the job done. Any job. If it was a sofa the client wanted, a sofa the client would have. And the morning after that, he would be in the Canary Islands, in Las Palmas, where a familiar bar and waitress would be waiting for him…

'What about my commission?' asked Leinonen, snapping Otto out of his reverie. 'For the information and the damage?'

He turned his head, showed Otto the holes in his bloody cheek. The grandfather clock struck the hour. The sound was dull and stuffy.

'I'll have to tie you up,' said Otto.

'What?' said Leinonen.

'Just for a few days,' Otto nodded and looked around.

His attention was drawn to the specially lit Christmas section of the warehouse – *Is there anything there I can use to tie him up?* – and didn't see the man called Leinonen hurtling towards him before it was too late. As he leapt forwards, Leinonen hurled a heavy metal bowl, and Otto heard the same kind of clang inside his head as he had from the grandfather clock. He lost his balance and fell on his back. Leinonen was battering him with the metal bowl now, pounding his face. Fine, thought Otto; he had suggested a neutral solution to the situation, he had tried to be friendly, he had offered friendship, but this man had rejected him. With his left hand, Otto managed to grip the set of sparkling Christmas lights hanging overhead. With the metal bowl still beating against his forehead, he sat up, thrust his right hand between his attacker's legs and clenched. Leinonen shouted and lowered the metal bowl but didn't drop it altogether. Otto staggered to his feet, pressed himself against Leinonen and quickly slung the Christmas lights around his neck, first once, then twice. Otto tightened his grip on the lights until the metal bowl clattered to the floor and Otto's arms were numb and all he could hear was the sound of his own panting. Then he pushed Leinonen into a dark-green armchair, took a deep breath, and as

Leinonen sat slumped in the old recliner – his cheeks glowing gnome-red, the Christmas lights flickering around his neck, his eyes staring at the ceiling – Otto thought he looked like someone whose passion for Christmas was so great, it had become his downfall. Otto touched first his nose, then his forehead. The bleeding wasn't very heavy, but he was bleeding all the same. But a little rough and tumble didn't annoy him as much as what had happened. Wasn't he already late? Why had this man had to stall him so long? He spotted a sack nearby, among the clutter of objects in the Christmas section of the warehouse. He picked it up and opened it. It was full of carefully wrapped presents. He wiped his nose and forehead, his sweaty neck, and looked at the grandfather clock that had just chimed. Maybe the situation wasn't completely hopeless after all, he thought.

He would catch up with the driver and the sofa before they reached Kouvola.

But one thing was certain: from now on, he would not be nearly as friendly.

4

On a dark winter's evening, the service station looked like a bright planet against the black canvas of outer space. And the figure that Ilmari Nieminen had heard, then seen a few metres to his right was, in some way, like a creature from outer space. Ilmari realised that this impression was partly due to the large sports bag in the man's hand, which appeared so heavy that he was doubled over with its weight.

Ilmari flinched, felt a flicker inside him. There was something familiar about this man, and, as unlikely as it seemed, Ilmari concluded that he must know him.

'Just because your father had a Thames,' he began, 'it doesn't necessarily mean you know how to mend one.'

'Back inside, I heard you were heading north,' the man continued as if he hadn't heard Ilmari's question. 'So am I. If I fix your van, you can give me a lift.'

'I'm not taking the most direct route,' said Ilmari.

'I'm not in a hurry,' the figure replied, and now Ilmari finally recognised the tone of voice, the manner of speech.

The bright lights of the service station glowed behind the figure, but little by little Ilmari began to make out the details. As he had suspected, the figure was around his age – about thirty-five, give or take – he had sharp, piercing eyes, slender but soft features and blond hair, short, tangled and partially standing on end. He was wearing a light-brown suede jacket with a thick lining, black baggy trousers and large, white basketball trainers that seemed unsuitable for the time of year. Ilmari could well have imagined that he was looking at Sting, who for one reason or another had found himself at a service station in northern Helsinki and could suddenly speak fluent Finnish. But Ilmari didn't imagine this. Now he knew whom he was looking at with absolute certainty.

'Antero Kuikka,' he said.

Filled with the noise of the traffic, the pause lasted perhaps two seconds, then the figure nodded.

'Ilmari Nieminen.'

They both took a step forwards, reaching out their hands. Ilmari calculated that it had been almost exactly twenty-three years since they had last shaken hands. At the same moment, Ilmari remembered other things. Good things at first, but straight afterwards a bad thing. Still, he didn't want to dwell on the events of their boyhood any further and returned to what they were doing and why. There wasn't any time to lose.

'A Phillips screwdriver and a set of pliers?' Ilmari asked.

'Ask for a pair of cutters too, just to be on the safe side.'

'Why don't you ask them yourself?'

'The same assistant has already thrown me out twice today, for not buying anything after my morning coffee. I can't afford a second cup. I doubt he's going to change his mind and suddenly start lending me their tools. I'm an unwelcome guest. And not just here.'

There was something exceptional about the way Antero Kuikka expressed these things, but something familiar too. He didn't beat around the bush, let alone try to hide things. He simply stated the truth. And this is exactly what he had done twenty-three years ago too.

Ilmari made his decision.

He walked back into the garage, explained the situation, left one of the banknotes he'd got from Leinonen on the counter as a deposit, borrowed the tools and returned to the van. He opened the passenger door, and Antero swung himself onto the floor of the cab in a single, smooth movement that looked like a combination of practice and natural agility. Then Antero asked Ilmari to hand him the tools, like a surgeon at an operating table.

Around ten minutes later, Antero slid out from the cab with the same easy, gymnastic movement and asked Ilmari to try the engine. Ilmari walked round the Thames, sat down and turned the key in the ignition. The van started, and Ilmari switched on the windscreen wipers.

They worked.

'A lift up north would be nice,' Ilmari heard beside him. 'Like I said, I'm in no hurry.'

Ilmari returned the tools to the garage, got his money back and walked back to the van, where he found Antero Kuikka rummaging in his large sports bag. The bag was on the snow-covered ground in front of the back door, and inside the bag Ilmari saw not only clothes but a surprising collection of cassettes. There might have been more cassettes than clothes. Ilmari couldn't quite work out what this said about his old childhood friend and travelling companion to be.

'It's a long journey,' said Antero. 'We're going to need some music. Any requests?'

Ilmari was about to say it didn't matter; all that mattered was that they got going. Then he thought of the length of the journey and remembered what it had felt like to drive to Kuopio, trapped in a car for hours, to the soundtrack of Kake Randelin's greatest hits.

'I prefer golden oldies myself,' said Ilmari. 'Sometimes new things, but mostly older music.'

Antero stopped rummaging and looked at Ilmari as if fitting him for a suit. This took a while.

'I should have guessed,' Antero said at last. 'The Rolling Stones, Led Zeppelin, Bowie, Lou Reed and early Rod Stewart, before he sold himself out.'

'Something like that,' said Ilmari. 'Maybe.'

'I've got all of those,' Antero nodded. 'And some newer stuff too. If you're into music, you can't stick with old fogies' bands forever.'

Ilmari said nothing. Antero continued rummaging, zipped up his bag and stood upright, a pile of cassette tapes in his arms. Ilmari opened the back door; with his free hand, Antero gripped the handles of his bag and was about to lift it into the back of the van when he stopped in his tracks. The highway hummed. The moment probably didn't last as long as it felt.

'Nice sofa,' said Antero after a pause.

'I'm delivering it to Kilpisjärvi,' said Ilmari. 'Via Ilomantsi and Vaasa.'

Still, Antero did not move. 'Not the most direct route,' he commented.

'I'll explain once we're on the road,' said Ilmari.

Antero finally lifted his bag into the back of the van, and Ilmari closed the door. They both turned slightly, and stood facing each other. Ilmari could see that about half of the cassettes in Antero's hands were ones he'd taped himself, and the other half were official releases. He quickly concluded that the collection didn't give any great cause for concern.

'Who chooses first?' asked Antero.

'You go ahead,' said Ilmari.

A moment later, Ilmari was wondering whether he ought to have paid more attention to the choice of music after all. As he steered the van onto Pakilantie, the ominous clang of 'Hell's Bells' rang from the loudspeaker. There was something foreboding about those bells, something akin to the service-station assistant's weather forecast, something unsuitable under the circumstances. He couldn't work out why he thought this. He had known this band for a long time, and he particularly enjoyed their early output. Ilmari was about to ask whether they might reconsider the choice of music, but Antero spoke before he had the chance.

'Christ,' said Antero as they crossed a bridge over the traffic flowing along the Ring Road. 'That old Saab 96v must be doing at least 140.'

Ilmari heard the clamour of the bells and the foreboding guitar pushing their way into the car and saw the small, dark-green Saab speeding under the bridge and continuing east, an angry cloud of snow billowing behind it. Ilmari slowed a little, stopped at the traffic lights, flicked the indicator and glanced once more towards the Ring Road. The lights changed, and he followed the downward curve of the slip road. Even going downhill, the Thames had trouble picking up speed, but it eventually reached the speed limit as they entered the flow of traffic.

'I don't mean to complain,' said Antero Kuikka after they had passed Pihlajanmäki on their right and Pukinmäki on their left, and the singer in the loudspeakers growled about the approaching storm, 'but given how far you're going, and in fact in general, your choice of vehicle is interesting, to say the least.'

'I didn't choose it myself,' said Ilmari. 'And I did promise you an explanation once we got going.'

Ilmari explained the course of events. His colleague from the sorting office in Pasila, an older man by the name of Riekkonen, had been offered a job on the side, which he'd initially accepted. But then Riekkonen had fallen ill, so he'd offered the job to Ilmari instead, because, after a short conversation at a bar, he knew Ilmari needed the money. (Which led Ilmari to tell Antero a short – a *very* short – version of his current situation and the financial pressures he was under.) He continued, saying he had called the number he'd been given and received detailed instructions, as well as – and this, Ilmari was keen to stress – answers to his questions. And so far, everything had been going to plan. He was on his way to Kilpisjärvi with the sofa in the back and some petrol money in his pocket.

Antero paused a while before saying, 'What were your questions? What did you ask?'

'First of all, I asked if I was doing anything illegal. Obviously.'

'Are you?'

Ilmari shook his head. 'Besides,' he continued, 'I'd already concluded that if I *was* doing anything illegal, this would be the wrong direction. If someone really wanted to smuggle goods, I'd be travelling the opposite way. Helsinki is where people make money. If you've smuggled drugs into Helsinki, there's no point then transporting them somewhere where the price is lower.'

'True.'

'And it's the same with any kind of contraband.'

'Also true.'

'Then,' Ilmari continued, 'I obviously asked why they can't transport the sofa themselves or why they don't use a removal company.'

'And what was the answer?'

'A family disagreement, apparently,' said Ilmari. 'This was the only method of transportation that everybody could agree on. I said I understood – family members often see things very differently.'

'I would have said the same,' Antero sighed.

Ilmari steered them first onto Lahdentie, then onto the motorway to Porvoo. The speed limit on the motorway was a hundred kilometres per hour. It very quickly became apparent that the maximum speed the Thames could deal with was just under ninety kilometres per hour, perhaps closer to eighty.

Anything above this made the motor rev too much, and the van started trembling, shaking, jolting, making it hard to control. Ilmari decided he'd said enough about himself and why he was on this journey; he had said everything that it was reasonable to say. In his travelling companion, he had a mechanic who could ensure they got where they were going and who had already done him a huge favour, which it was only fair to repay. He'd now done so by telling Antero the story behind this trip, and didn't feel he needed to say any more. But this wasn't the only reason that Ilmari now fell silent. He was waiting for Antero Kuikka to say something about himself, to tell him some of what had happened between their years playing football together as boys and their encounter at the petrol station in Pakila. With every minute that passed, Ilmari recalled more about Antero. He remembered that, though they had never been proper friends, they had been able to read each other's movements on the pitch and at times played together almost seamlessly. For one reason or another.

The streetlights suddenly came to an end, and they dived into the darkness and the swirling snow. Ilmari had to slow down as his visibility was reduced almost to zero.

'Family business for me too,' Antero said eventually. 'That's why I'm heading up north. So I really appreciate the ride. More than you can know. I don't know how I would have got to Rovaniemi otherwise. There's no one I could have asked for money. I've only got a small pension, and it's always gone long before the end of the month.'

Ilmari almost jerked in surprise, but he managed not to turn the wheel, not to make the van jolt. But it was a close call. He glanced to the side once more to check that he hadn't been seeing things or reached the wrong conclusions. No, he had not been seeing things and had not reached the wrong conclusions: sitting in the passenger seat was the very same Antero Kuikka, who was exactly the same age as him. Noticing his quick glance, Antero took the black leather glove from his left hand, clenched his fist and tapped his shin. The sound was like someone knocking at a door. Ilmari had a vision of someone about to open up.

'I was working on the railways,' said Antero. 'A train ran over my leg. Left it there, on the tracks.'

Ilmari waited, expecting Antero to continue, but he didn't.

Just then, the van was filled with the silence between songs. The Thames hummed.

'I'm sorry,' said Ilmari once the music resumed. He remembered how smoothly Antero had moved, how agile he'd looked as he swung himself onto the floor of the van's cab, and he was about to ask about it when Antero spoke.

'But that's enough about me,' he said. 'Why are we going to Ilomantsi?'

5

As Erkki Liljalampi's egg-yolk-yellow Lada 1200 turned into Kustaankatu, Anneli Kukkorinne's suspicions reared their head once more. Was Erkki Liljalampi still a communist – really, truly, and with all his heart?

Anneli gripped the fake-leather handles of the bulky, cumbersome suitcase she had been given as a gift during a visit to East Germany and lifted it from the crusted, icy pavement. She watched the Lada approach and tried to decide what she saw, or what she thought she saw.

Was Erkki slowing on the hill or not?

Of course, she could hear the Lada was revving its way up the hill, but that didn't necessarily tell her the whole story. The car wasn't travelling very fast given their schedule. And the reason for crawling along like that couldn't be that Erkki didn't know how to drive a car; he had been driving trucks for nearly forty years before his recent retirement.

The Lada eventually arrived, and even from where she stood, outside the car, Anneli could hear Erkki pulling the hand brake. It sounded like a large spring being stretched to its limit. Anneli opened the back door, and a thick cloud of unfiltered cigarette smoke billowed into the frigid Kallio evening. She placed the suitcase in the footwell behind the front seats – there was plenty of space because there was only one item in the back of the car: a green, unopened pack of North State cigarettes – closed the door, then sat down in the passenger seat. Erkki put the car in gear, and they set off. At least, in theory. They slowly climbed to the top of the hill, where Erkki took the car out of gear and allowed them to free-wheel down the other side.

'What's going on?' asked Anneli and looked over at Erkki. His blue-grey eyes stared straight ahead, his twitching cheek muscles suggesting he was gritting his teeth.

'Saving petrol,' he said. 'Got to pay for it myself.'

Once they reached Aleksis Kivi Street, Erkki gently pressed the accelerator, and through a series of slow corners and what could only be called slow accelerations, they eventually reached Hämeentie and were on their way east to Ilomantsi, as per the Secretary's instructions. Everything was in order – or at least things were going to plan. But Anneli again felt that this wasn't the case.

'We will catch up with that car, won't we?' she asked.

'By Lappeenranta, I guess,' said Erkki, and took another drag on his green North State cigarette. 'By Imatra, at the latest. He's in an old English van; we've got a fine socialist sports car.'

Anneli had a strong sense of unease, but she couldn't quite put her finger on what was causing it. She and Erkki had been working operations together for years, but now there was definitely something off about him. It wasn't that he was thirty years her senior; it was something to do with his attitude, and even then, only a very subtle shift of emphasis. A shift that it was impossible to pin down, because Erkki wasn't one for nuance; his tone of voice was the same no matter what he was talking about, and it was impossible to say when he was being sincere or when he was being sarcastic, if he ever indulged in such a thing. And because of this, Erkki's monotone awoke a familiar sense of trust and fresh suspicions all at once.

Erkki filled his lungs with smoke. Anneli looked at his rock-hewn features and thought perhaps she understood what this was all about after all. In fact, Erkki had already mentioned it.

'You're irritated that you have to pay for the petrol yourself,' she said.

'It's annoying,' said Erkki.

'I've told you a hundred times,' she exclaimed. 'We all have to make little sacrifices to achieve the greater good. We have an important mission. This is about something far bigger than us. It's about the whole world, the future. And one day, even the petrol you put in your car will be free.'

They had reached the end of Hämeentie, the spot where the road widened and turned into the highway to Lahti. The Lada gathered speed – slowly. Snow slapped against the windscreen as though someone were driving the blizzard towards them with a giant leaf blower. Anneli didn't know why the Secretary had, yet again, asked her and Erkki to form a hit squad. Not that she was complaining, let alone questioning the Secretary's decisions or their consistency. The Secretary knew what he was doing and received his instructions from the highest possible authority.

'We're going to miss *Dallas*,' said Erkki out of the blue.

It took Anneli a moment to realise Erkki wasn't talking about their route but the television show. Which Anneli had only watched once, and even then, under duress.

'Good,' she scoffed. 'Imperialist rubbish. Of course, in a way it's instructional. It shows how rotten and decadent America really is. Money is the only thing that matters to them.'

'They're in the oil business,' said Erkki.

'Who?' asked Anneli.

'The Ewings,' Erkki replied. 'It just occurred to me when you mentioned free petrol.'

'But in America, it isn't free,' said Anneli. 'In America, nothing is free. The capitalists make sure of that. A system like that can't last forever. Sooner or later, it'll reach the end of the road.'

Erkki paused for a moment.

'Still, I hope they don't stop *Dallas*,' he said eventually.

Anneli was about to say that she couldn't imagine a scenario in which the revolution would first wipe the materialists off the face of the earth, their bodies weakened with fast food and their brains addled with mindless entertainment, only to allow them, somehow, to continue churning out propaganda for the consumption of the newly emboldened proletariat. But she stopped herself, reminding herself that Erkki hadn't delved into the cause, its ideas and theories, in quite the same way she had. He was, and always had been, far too fixated on practical considerations, and this only narrowed a person's understanding of what was possible. Anneli decided to let it go. Besides, right this minute, she had other, more pressing, things to worry about.

'Are you clear about what we're doing and why we're following that van?' she asked.

'More or less,' said Erkki.

'And...?'

'We're going to reappropriate what is being transported in the back of the van,' he said. 'Then, one way or another, we're going to transport it ourselves from that point onwards.'

'And why are we only *temporarily* reappropriating the cargo?' asked Anneli.

'Because,' Erkki began, 'the cargo, an antique sofa, is very valuable. The cause needs money, and we are going to get our hands on some.'

'Correct,' said Anneli. 'Except that the more correct and more just formulation would be, of course, that in the current consumerist media environment, the only way to raise awareness to levels required for the forthcoming revolution is to fight propaganda with the truth, and to do that, we must turn the capitalists' most devious weapon – money – against them.'

Erkki lit another green North State and filled his lungs with the industrial smoke. Anneli waited a moment for him to say something, but he seemed to be concentrating on the road and his cigarette.

'And once we have acquired the sofa,' she continued, 'why are we going to transfer it to another vehicle and not simply commandeer their van while we're at it?'

'Because the people who have been driving the van will probably report it stolen,' Erkki replied. 'And we don't want to be arrested for stealing a car. And even if they don't report it stolen, we need to do everything we can to avoid being identified.'

Anneli turned and looked at the road ahead.

'What about the glove compartment?' she asked. 'Does it contain what I asked for?'

'It does,' said Erkki.

Anneli opened the glove compartment and nodded, satisfied that Erkki was telling the truth.

'Where did you get it?'

'From a trusted source,' he said.

A thought flashed through Anneli's mind: perhaps Erkki hadn't lost his touch after all. She took the pistol out of the glove compartment. She felt the weight of it in her hand, checked the magazine, and aimed at the motorway in front of her. Then she returned the weapon to the compartment and closed the door. She was about to thank Erkki for getting the pistol, but he spoke first.

'Violence is never the answer,' he said. 'I suggest we don't resort to using the pistol while taking control of the sofa.'

Anneli looked at him, his granite profile, and all she could see were shadows in the rockface.

'We're not stealing anything,' she said. 'We're doing the opposite: we are returning something to shared ownership, where it will be used for the greatest good imaginable.'

Erkki raised his cigarette to his lips, took a drag.

'According to the Secretary,' he said, slowly blowing the smoke from his lungs, 'we should be able to break the lock on the back of the van in under a minute, and after that it will be plain sailing. And the driver is a bungling amateur.'

Anneli thought about this for a moment, then shrugged her shoulders.

'This will be a quick and easy assignment,' she said.

She heard Erkki put his foot on the accelerator and, after a short delay, felt the Lada slowly increase its speed.

6

Antero was asleep. Ilmari wasn't especially surprised; Antero had been waiting for a lift for a long time. He hadn't spent just the previous day at the petrol station but the night before that too – on only one cup of coffee. Antero said that hunger didn't much bother him; as he put it, he had embraced the 'Stoic lifestyle' years ago, in the aftermath of his accident. *Some things are within our control, some are not*. Stoicism had taught him how to draw a distinction between impressions and facts, and to toughen himself in other respects too.

Ilmari had kept their speed slow, but the unavoidable truth was that the Thames guzzled petrol regardless. They would soon have to stop, hopefully at Imatra, which they were now approaching and where there was a greater chance of finding a petrol station that was still open. The snow had paused, and in the darkened landscape the city lights looked like a small but persistent lamp beneath a large blanket. During the course of the trip, Ilmari had listened to The Rolling Stones' *Exile on Main St* double album, then put on some Peter Tosh, and had just made an interesting discovery: a mix tape Antero had recorded.

He was about to press the cassette into the tape player when the yellow shell at the petrol station appeared, shining like an overheated sun between the black spruces lining the road. He returned the cassette to its box, turned his head and saw a man fast asleep.

'Let's have a cup of coffee,' said Ilmari.

'I still don't have enough money,' Antero replied immediately, his eyes closed.

'I have,' said Ilmari. 'Enough for two cups.'

It was true. Ilmari was beginning to understand the Thames's fuel consumption, he knew how much money he had been given for the petrol costs and he knew the approximate length of the journey. Some simple division, multiplication and addition told him that he could spare enough money for two cups of petrol-station coffee.

Antero opened his eyes. Ilmari turned onto the slip road, engine-braked and shifted down a gear. They turned another two times and ended up in the forecourt outside the petrol station. Ilmari steered the car to one of the pumps, then switched off the engine. It felt as though the whole world had momentarily stopped spinning. The Thames was the only vehicle by the pumps. The café inside looked empty.

Antero slid out of the car, and Ilmari pulled on his gloves. Once outside, he gripped the icy pump handle, started filling up the tank and watched out of the corner of his eye as Antero made his way into the café. He was using a walking stick now. His gait was surprisingly smooth. The tank filled, Ilmari screwed the lid back in place and walked towards the café. Then something – he wasn't sure what – made him stop and look around. Nobody in sight. He continued on his way, stepped inside, went into the bathroom and held his frozen hands under the hot, invigorating water for a moment, then returned to the shop and paid for the petrol and the two cups of coffee that Antero had already carried over to a table by the window. He sat down opposite Antero, saw the front of the Thames to the right and gave an involuntarily smile. Maybe the Thames would make it after all.

'I fell asleep halfway through your story,' said Antero. 'You were telling me why we're going to Ilomantsi.'

'My aunt lives there,' said Ilmari. 'And I promised to go and change the batteries in her torch.'

Antero's expression didn't flinch. 'I don't mean to spoil a good plan,' he began, 'but couldn't she have found help from someone a little closer to home? So you wouldn't have to drive all the way from Helsinki just to change a few batteries?'

'It's not really about the batteries,' said Ilmari. 'It's because, well, my aunt practically raised me, and when I was little I always wanted to change the batteries in her torch. At some point we agreed that this would be my job from now on and that I'd always come and do it for her. I haven't been to change them for a while, and now I promised I would.'

Antero sat in silence, stirring a third sugar cube into his coffee. Ilmari sipped his own. It tasted burnt, but somehow still weak.

'Hats off, my friend,' said Antero.

'For what?'

'Keeping your promises. It's important,' Antero continued. 'I haven't always been able to do it myself.'

Ilmari tried to work out whether there was any subtext to what Antero had said, but he couldn't read between the lines.

'You can start anytime,' he said.

'What made you start?'

Ilmari was starting to feel awkward. Which was a shame, because he had come to like the simple idea that he had managed to pick up a mechanic and a bag full of music to keep him company. In fact, the combination had felt rather pleasant. He hadn't been at all bothered by the fact that Antero had essentially slept all the way to Imatra.

'It's just,' Ilmari began, 'I know what it feels like when people don't keep their promises. I want to be different. Especially when it comes to my daughter.'

Antero tasted his coffee. Perhaps it was his Stoicism, but it was impossible to tell what he thought of this coffee, which tasted like a fusion of old tyres and an even older kettle grill.

'What have you promised her?' Antero asked eventually.

'A piano,' said Ilmari.

'A piano?'

'I'm going to collect it from the instrument store on Aleksanterinkatu before Christmas,' Ilmari nodded.

'That's only a few days away.'

'It's open until midday on Christmas Eve,' said Ilmari. 'I'll have plenty of time.'

Antero looked like he was about to say something but decided against it. He drank his coffee; he even seemed to like it. Ilmari swallowed his own considerably more slowly.

'Can I ask you something?' said Antero.

Ilmari looked at him more closely, mostly to see whether he was serious. In the last fifteen minutes, Antero had asked him countless questions. But Antero appeared to be deadly serious. His slender face was serious, his Sting haircut jutting upwards. Ilmari decided that, after he'd answered Antero's next question, he would ask one of his own. He gesticulated: please, go ahead.

'Have you ever thought about ... what happened back then?' asked Antero.

Ilmari had thought he was prepared for any question, but this startled him. He had finished his coffee. He glanced out at the van and was about to say something – he didn't quite know what – when he instantly forgot both the question and, in fact, Antero himself.

He saw movement by the back door of the van. There was someone there. Ilmari stood up.

'You don't have to answer,' Antero said quickly. 'Raking over the past isn't really my thing...'

'Let's talk about this later,' said Ilmari and started towards the door.

As Ilmari stepped out into the frozen evening, he saw a sleeve or a hat disappear behind the van and heard the sound of metal being twisted. Then he heard another car's horn and, soon afterwards, the car itself. He didn't see the car; it must have been behind one of the many tall verges of snow piled up around the edges of the forecourt. But he did see a figure in a puffy jacket and a balaclava running towards those snow verges and disappearing behind them. Arriving at the van, Ilmari saw that the lock on the back door had been broken and the doors left ajar. He heard a car door slam shut behind the verges and the car speed away. He turned, started running. He went around the snow verges and reached the road but couldn't see the car. To his left, the road sloped downwards and curved into the distance, but all was quiet in that direction. Too quiet. To his right was an empty crossroads with loose snow still fluttering in the light of the streetlamps. That's where the car must have gone, either behind the rows of apartment blocks or the Co-op. For half a fleeting second, Ilmari thought he should give pursuit but decided this was futile. He stood in the middle of the road, thought about what he had seen, then walked back to the Thames where Antero was waiting for him.

'The lock's been forced open,' said Antero. 'Now we won't be able to shut it.'

Ilmari examined the lock, then looked up at Antero.

'Were these your friends?' he asked.

Antero's expression never changed, even when he was asleep, but now a flicker of something suddenly crossed his face.

'Pardon me?'

They looked each other in the eyes. Ilmari said nothing.

Antero eventually broke the stalemate. 'I got in your van at the petrol station in Pakila,' he said. 'By which point you already had the van, the sofa and the route. I didn't know anything about any of that.'

The frozen air stung Ilmari's fingers, but he could feel something ablaze inside him.

'What do you think just happened?' he asked.

'You want me to speculate?'

'Unless that would go against your Stoic principles,' Ilmari retorted.

Ilmari had chosen his words quickly but precisely. He could see that they had an effect on Antero.

'Very well,' said Antero. 'The sofa is valuable. Anyone can see that. Someone must have peered in through the window and decided they wanted to take the sofa for themselves. They began by breaking the lock. They must have assumed we would stay in the café a while longer, perhaps have a bite to eat. They weren't to know that we can't afford that. I didn't see the car that sped away, so for that reason I can't tell whether the idea was to transfer the sofa into that vehicle, but I imagine that was probably the thieves' intention. It would make sense. If they had taken our vehicle, it would be easy for us to report it stolen. But because we didn't see the other vehicle, it would be much harder for us to tell the police what to look out for.'

Ilmari kept his eyes fixed on Antero, then nodded. 'That's what I thought too,' he admitted, and decided that, as far as Antero was concerned, this was the end of the matter. He'd found out what he needed to know – he was satisfied that Antero wasn't involved in what had just happened – and he was about to work out how to solve the next problem when Antero interrupted him.

'Seems you still don't have many friends,' he said.

Ilmari stopped in his tracks. 'What's that supposed to mean?'

'Something happens that's a bit difficult or uncomfortable, and even though it has nothing to do with the people around you, you start blaming them for the problem and insult them in the most profound and personal way.'

The flames inside Ilmari rose from the pit of his stomach to his eyes.

'I'm not the one who stole the camping donations,' he said, staring at Antero.

There it was. He hadn't intended to return to events from twenty-three years ago, but now it was done. Ilmari sighed. One sentence had brought back the full chain of events in dazzling technicolour: the money that they had been collecting together for a long period of time, and which was supposed to go towards a camping trip to Vierumäki, a trip they had talked and dreamt about for months. The money's sudden, unexplained disappearance. The boys' suspicions of one another. The coach's decision, and the repercussions of that decision.

He suspected the same sequence had appeared in Antero's mind too.

'You think I was responsible for the money going missing, don't you,' said Antero, his intonation revealing that this was not meant as a question.

'Who else could it have been?'

'There were eleven players on the team,' said Antero.

'And we all agreed to Uimonen's interview. Except you.'

'Eleven players,' said Antero. 'And one coach.'

'Why didn't you agree to be interviewed?'

Antero didn't answer right away.

'The situation was unfair right from the start,' he replied eventually. 'By that point, the game was up.'

Antero ended there, and it sounded and felt like he had said all he was going to say on the subject.

The frigid air was doing its job; Ilmari's fingers were now tingling with pain. He felt like saying something else but, at the same time, he sensed that the worst of his agitation had abated. Besides, right now, a missed football camp several decades ago wasn't his top priority. He drew the cold air into his lungs.

'I'll go inside and find something we can use to keep the doors shut,' he said.

Antero said nothing. Ilmari walked off towards the petrol station.

Inside, it quickly became clear what he could afford and what he could not. He returned with a tangled ball of nylon string. First, he checked the fastenings holding the sofa in place. The ropes were still strong and firm. Then he and Antero tied the door handles together. They worked in silence, but as a team. The doors no longer shut properly, but using many lengths of string they managed to pull them almost closed, and from a distance it looked as though the doors were properly locked.

They returned to the main road. The snowfall had started again, and their visibility soon began to worsen. They did not say a word for a long while. Ilmari began to feel the need for some music.

'If you choose something,' he said, nodding at the bag of cassettes, 'I'll gladly listen.'

Antero said nothing and didn't move for a moment. Then he reached a hand into the bag, carefully took out a tape and pushed it into the player.

'*If you want blood, you got it...*'

7

Ilomantsi was like a frozen arsehole, thought Otto Puolanka: small, tight and ice cold. He took out his packet of Camels, lit a cigarette. The temperature inside the Saab was almost zero.

Otto understood the problem with small towns. Everybody knew everybody else, and anything unfamiliar quickly drew attention. That meant that he had to be careful, he had to keep a low profile. And this, in turn, was a problem when it came to gathering information. He knew that the sofa was either already here or on its way here, and he knew what kind of vehicle he was looking for. But he did not know why the sofa was here or why it was on its way here, and he couldn't ask, either. He couldn't ring every doorbell in Ilomantsi and ask whether someone was expecting an antique sofa, either as a permanent fixture or just as a temporary one, and whether he could wait for it with them.

And so, his only option was to look for and find it himself.

He had already driven around the town centre and hadn't seen any trace of the Thames or its determined driver. Now he was sitting by the side of a road that split the town in two, in the car park outside the supermarket, keenly following every passing vehicle.

Or trying to, at least.

There was a bar across the street, its two illuminated windows suggesting it was open. Otto had picked up five bottles of beer from the shop, but he didn't like this arrangement: he was sitting by himself in a cold, dark car drinking beer that was barely four-percent. Yet going to a bar was impossible. The regulars would all know one another. He would be noticed; in the worst-case scenario someone might even ask him something. Such as why he was in town and what he was doing there. The bar was out of the question. Keeping a low profile was his priority.

He smoked his Camels, drank his bottle of Lahti Blue, followed the passing cars.

Fifteen minutes later, he had an idea:

Why shouldn't he go to the bar? After all, a bar is traditionally the kind of place where people share information, particularly in an unofficial capacity. There's always a warm, friendly atmosphere in bars; that's why people go there. It's easy to start talking to strangers in a bar, and people pay hardly any attention to what others say or ask. Thinking about it, the bar is the best possible solution to his Ilomantsi problem – to this whole charade around the sofa. And where better to keep a low profile than in a dimly lit, smoke-filled bar? Otto shook his head, wondered why he had made such a mountain out of a molehill, and started the engine.

He parked outside the cooperative bank next to the bar. He knew from experience that you could never be too careful. Not that he needed to take particular precautions right now. His mood had already picked up considerably, and once he stepped into the bar he felt better still. There was only one other customer, a man in a woolly hat sitting near the counter at the other end of the room. The barman was reading the evening tabloid. But the thing that most cheered Otto up was the jukebox. If it had his new favourite song, that would give him the boost he needed.

He walked up to the counter; the barman raised his eyes. Otto nodded and pointed to the Karjala tap, got a pint of beer and, with this in hand, walked over to a table by the window where he could still look out at the road bisecting the town, but from the opposite side. At least now he wasn't alone in his cold, dark car. He was sitting in the warmth of the bar but was still able to keep an eye on the passing traffic. Why hadn't he thought of this sooner? Besides, everything was going as planned. The barman hadn't asked anything; in fact, he hadn't said a word throughout their entire interaction, and neither had Otto. The man in the woolly hat now looked like he had lost something under his table and that finding it would take some time. Otto took a sip of his pint, remembered the music and thought this might be a way to lighten the mood and make his upcoming enquiries sound a bit more natural.

He took some coins from his jacket pocket and walked up to the jukebox. He found the song he was looking for, selected it and immediately felt the blood warming in his veins, pumping a little faster.

'Eye of the Tiger'.

Otto returned to his table and again thought of the best film he had ever seen. *Rocky III*. He'd seen it twice at the pictures.

Otto wasn't usually one for smiling, but now he started cautiously moving his head in time with the music and glanced over at the man in the woolly hat. He wasn't searching for something anymore. He was staring at Otto. Otto nodded to the music more forcefully now, hoping it might have an effect on this one other customer. The song ended, the man in the woolly hat got up and walked over to the jukebox. A sluggish, melancholic song started playing. The man in the woolly hat looked at him.

When the song came to an end, Otto stood up. He needed another blast of 'Eye of the Tiger', and fast. But the man in the woolly hat was sitting nearer to the jukebox, and he got there first.

His coin slid into the machine just as Otto reached it. The man in the woolly hat turned, and the same miserable crooning started up again.

They stood opposite each other, both listening to the depressing dirge.

Then the man in the woolly hat turned again, this time more slowly, as though he thought he had won something. He walked to the end of the bar, and from there into the toilet.

Otto stood in front of the jukebox for a moment then followed the man.

It seemed the man had been expecting this. As Otto opened the toilet door, the man punched him. Or tried to, at least. Otto ducked, then headbutted the man as he lunged forwards, producing a sound like a layer of cartilage being pushed through a meat grinder. The man raised both hands to his face and staggered backwards. Otto grabbed the fire extinguisher from the wall, stepped into the toilet and, with the extinguisher, knocked the hat from the man's head. The man slumped into the urinal. Otto pushed the extinguisher's hose into the man's mouth, pulled out the plug, pressed the handle, then held the man's head in place and filled his mouth with foam.

"'Eye of the Tiger'", said Otto.

He put down the extinguisher, shook the foam from his heavy winter boots – both the toilet and the man were covered in it – and returned to the bar. He walked past the barman, who had been sitting next to the still-moaning jukebox throughout the incident, and even now didn't look up from the news of the latest murders.

Otto walked out to his car, cracked opened another Lahti Blue, and felt a strange, nagging sensation inside him.

8

Ilmari took more than one wrong turning before they eventually found the right house, a little over two kilometres from the centre of Ilomantsi, in the depths of the woods. His aunt had put a candle by the roadside so that he would find the right turning. And when he steered the car into the short driveway, they saw two lights on the front wall. They drove towards the rectangular log cabin, its timbers painted a deep red, and pulled up in front of it. Ilmari switched off the engine, and one sound was replaced by another.

The dog that had appeared in front of the car was black and the size of a horse, and its barking and growling resembled those of a prehistoric monster more than of a pet. It rose up on its hind legs, thumped its front paws against the windscreen and eyed them malevolently. It looked at both of them in turn, baring its teeth. Ilmari estimated that its head was around the size of an elk's and that, though it didn't have antlers, it did have antler-sized teeth.

Antero didn't look especially startled, but neither did he look like he was in a hurry to step out of the van. During the latter part of their journey, they hadn't returned to the events of the past, and Ilmari felt as though they had switched to other topics by common, if unspoken, agreement. Not that the conversation had been particularly lively. For the most part, they had stuck to talking about music. It had turned out that Antero's tape collection was a leftover from his short stint working at the Discus record shop in Helsinki, where his wages were paid in music.

The dog was growling and drooling, and looked like it intended first to rip them to shreds and only then to get to know them better. Then, Ilmari's aunt appeared in the garden – 'Puppe,' she called – and the monster turned into the sweetest lapdog: it immediately backed away from the front of the van and trotted to its owner's side, wagging its sabre-like tail.

Ilmari opened the Thames's door, and Aunt Maria hugged him in her usual perfunctory manner, in which her tight squeeze and almost immediate dismissal felt equally important. As she did so, she noticed Ilmari's travelling companion. Ilmari saw the confusion on both his aunt's face and Antero's. He understood why. Antero probably hadn't expected to see such a flamboyant elderly lady in the middle of the almost impassable woods, and his aunt certainly hadn't expected to see anyone other than Ilmari. But this didn't seem to be the only thing that had taken her by surprise.

'I didn't know that you had friends,' she said, addressing Ilmari but speaking loudly enough that even the trees at the end of the garden could hear her.

Ilmari felt ill at ease. He was about to deny this or at the very least ask her to explain what she meant, but he quickly decided against doing so. He hadn't come here to disagree with her. He had come to tell her something. He just had to find the right moment to say it. This wasn't it.

'Aunt Maria,' he said instead, then introduced his aunt and his travelling companion to each other: 'This is Antero.'

He added that he and Antero used to play football together, that they had bumped into each other today after twenty-three years and that Antero had been able to fix a problem with the van. Antero and his aunt greeted each other and looked at least a little pleased to have met. Ilmari was about to say something about their journey and that they were rather tired; it had been

a long drive, and it might be a good idea if they could rest first
and only then—

'If you could just give me a hand with the logs,' his aunt
interjected. This didn't sound like a suggestion or a question so
much as a statement of what was about to happen. 'Before your
pea soup. That would be smashing.'

They felled a birch under the starry sky. Ilmari used a chainsaw
for the first time in years. Antero didn't complain once. He didn't
ask why they were cutting down a tree on a dark evening and
didn't even mention his hunger. He found it hard to move
around in the deep snow but always managed to be in the right
place at the right time, nevertheless. Ilmari chopped and
trimmed, Antero gathered and tidied. Ilmari knew this wasn't
just about the firewood. His aunt wanted to make something
clear. Like she had always done.

They returned to the garden hungry and exhausted, yet
curiously invigorated, only to see that Ilmari's aunt had heated
up the sauna for them. They bathed in the ninety-degree outdoor
sauna, lay down in the snow to cool off, made snow angels.
Antero's angel was missing the lower part of its right wing.

Inside the house, they were served bowls of pea soup. The soup
was thick, the chunks of smoky ham melted in their mouths.
Both added dollops of mustard and ate long slices of ryebread
spread with a thick layer of butter. Ilmari's aunt drank coffee at
the other end of the table. Ilmari took in his surroundings and
thought that everything looked almost as it had in the past:
minimal, deliberate – beautiful in its simplicity. As though every
item, every piece of furniture, had finally found the exact location
it had always been looking for.

Twice, Ilmari found himself glancing at his aunt. The first
time, he might have looked at her without her noticing. He still

didn't know what had made his aunt move all the way out here, but he suspected it had something to do with her relationships. Everything did. His aunt was about twenty years older than him, and Ilmari knew they looked very similar – with one exception. With his aunt, everything was exaggerated: the darkness of her skin, her eyes, her hair, the contour of her nose and chin, the width of her mouth. She looked like an old European duchess on the silver screen, even when she was drinking instant coffee in the forests of eastern Finland, as she was now.

They had already talked about the journey, the van, touched on the subject of politics and the Soviet submarine that had run aground in Swedish waters, but not about anything personal. Not until Antero reminded them of the imminent Christmas holiday.

'Any plans?' asked Antero, deliberately aiming his words past Ilmari and towards the other end of the table. 'I can't see any signs of Christmas, no tree or decorations.'

'There's still a few days to go,' said Ilmari's aunt.

Antero nodded, apparently content with this answer, and scraped the last of his soup from the bottom of his bowl.

'What about you, Ilmari?' asked his aunt.

Ilmari explained his situation, telling his aunt that he planned to be – and intended to be – at the instrument store on Aleksanterinkatu on Christmas Eve.

'That's Ilmari's best quality,' she said. 'When he decides to do something, he does it.'

Ilmari waited, expecting Antero to ask what his worst qualities were – that would have been typical of Antero – but he sidestepped the matter entirely.

'Aren't you afraid, being out here alone?' he asked Ilmari's aunt with a nod towards the darkness outside. 'The bears, for instance?'

'The bears? They're already hibernating.'

'I meant, bear-like creatures, unwanted guests,' said Antero. 'People who turn up uninvited.'

'Uninvited, maybe,' said his aunt, 'but not entirely unexpected. If you know they exist.'

Antero looked like he was thinking about something. Perhaps about her response, or maybe something else.

'If they do come, what will you do?' he asked.

'Try to talk to them.'

'And if they don't listen to you, what will you do then?' he pressed. 'You and Puppe will go on the offensive?'

'Of course we won't,' she replied. 'It's his size that makes him look frightening. He's about as dangerous as the first butterfly in spring.' Then Ilmari's aunt raised her hand and pointed to a shelf near the ceiling behind Antero.

Antero turned. Ilmari looked up at the shelf. All three of them saw the same shotgun.

'It's a slightly larger calibre than usual,' said his aunt. 'It wouldn't quite make a hole in those timbers, but almost. After using that, my shoulder is bruised for a week.'

Antero stared at the shotgun, then turned back to face the table.

'Better a sore shoulder,' he began, 'than having to serve pea soup to any old rascal.'

Ilmari's aunt smiled. Antero smiled.

Ilmari had been hoping for a moment without Antero, but now Antero was taking seconds of soup. Another full bowl, which meant he would sit there spooning it into his mouth for a while yet. Ilmari didn't know where the soup and bread disappeared to; Antero was a scrawny, one-legged man. Ilmari decided there probably wouldn't be a better moment, or at least he wasn't prepared to wait for one. He would say what he had come to say, tell his aunt what had been weighing on his mind for so long. He wiped his mouth on the napkin, looked at his aunt.

'I know you still take care of me,' he began.

His aunt didn't seem surprised at his words or the change of subject. 'It's true,' she said.

'You don't have to,' he said. 'Everything is fine. Really.'

His aunt was silent. Half a second too long, he thought. Then she asked, 'Are you sure?'

'Yes,' said Ilmari. 'That's why I came. So you'd see for yourself.'

His aunt looked at him closely. Ilmari had to admit that his turning up here with an old van and strange travelling companion a few days before Christmas might not have been the best way to gain her trust. But he had done it because he cared about his aunt and felt that he owed her. Besides, everything *would* be fine, and very soon. So, in a way, and in the broadest sense, Ilmari was telling the truth.

'Very well,' his aunt said eventually.

Ilmari felt a degree of relief, but he also felt some embarrassment that Antero was sitting next to him witnessing this conversation between himself and his aunt. On the other hand, nothing about Antero suggested that he had been paying them much attention. He was eating his pea soup, regularly squeezing long stripes of mustard into it. He was eating like a man who hadn't eaten for days. Which was beginning to feel likely; he didn't even slow down when their pudding of pancakes arrived. He ate half a tray of them by himself, smearing them with Ilmari's aunt's strawberry jam and praising the combination, even calling it a heavenly experience. Perhaps even Stoics have their weaknesses, thought Ilmari. His aunt appeared thrilled at Antero's healthy appetite. This was what she was like, thought Ilmari: she understood hungry, damaged people.

The starry sky was clear and bright when Ilmari went out to check on the improvised lock on the back of the Thames. It wasn't a lock in the conventional sense. The string holding the back doors together was strong, though naturally not as strong as the original steel. Ilmari tested its strength with his hands, thought about what he had seen at the petrol station and still wasn't sure what it was all about. For some reason, neither he nor Antero had mentioned the incident at any point during the evening.

Puppe had followed him outside. Once the dog had been able to shove its enormous head into Ilmari's armpit and had had a good sniff, the dog had seemed to recognise him. Puppe pattered out into the garden and peed deep, steaming holes into the snow. Ilmari was about to go back indoors and was reaching towards the door handle when he noticed that Puppe wasn't following him anymore. The dog was no longer in the garden. He called out, but the dog didn't come running over. Ilmari returned to the van, looked around.

The snow-covered forest, the outhouse, the sauna, their snow angels.

Then he heard a growl.

Ilmari walked towards the growling and noticed that the beastly noise could be heard at quite a distance, for the simple reason that the source of the sound was so large and powerful. Puppe was standing at the end of the drive, where the outdoor candle was still burning. Ilmari saw from the dog's posture that it must have seen or heard something. He stopped about fifteen metres away and listened, but all he could hear was Puppe. He couldn't see any movement in the dark forest. The stars were twinkling, the outdoor candle flaring like a small, bright bonfire. The snow was by turns even and rippling, the woods as dark as the bottom of a well.

Ilmari walked up to the place where Puppe was standing. The snow crunched under his shoes; the sound echoed through the otherwise silent world. From the dog's black flanks and the position of its limbs, he could tell it was tensing its muscles. But it didn't race off anywhere. His aunt had trained it well. It guarded the gates, guarded its home.

Ilmari gazed out in the same direction as the dog. He gazed for a long while. Eventually, he couldn't tell whether he had seen something or whether it was something else altogether – his tired eyes, perhaps. But the feeling remained: it was as if he was being watched.

9

'Wakey wakey,' said Anneli Kukkorinne, prodding the crumpled sleeping bag on the back seat. 'The sun's already risen.'

There was more strength in her prod than was necessary to wake him, but it was, nevertheless, a calm, restrained version of what Anneli wanted to do. She hadn't forgotten or forgiven the complete failure of the day before. Erkki's failure. His stupid plan that was supposed to be founded on gradual advance, cunning and good groundwork – in this case the covert damage to the van's back doors so that, when they came to take control of the sofa, they could simply transfer it from one vehicle to another – but which had ended in near disaster and a very narrow escape at a petrol station on the outskirts of Imatra.

Anneli turned again, switched the binoculars to her left hand and hit the man curled in a foetal position in the sleeping bag on his lower back, just where she thought his kidney might be. Erkki Liljalampi let out a sound that resembled a cow's lowing, if the cow in question were also a chain-smoker.

'Sorry,' said Anneli. 'But we might need to hurry. I saw movement by the house.'

Erkki sat up, started coughing. He coughed again, then lit a North State.

'Hurry,' he said. Or asked.

'Today we're following *my* plan,' said Anneli. 'Enough of this "stage one, stage two, stage three" codswallop. Now we're going to take what is rightfully ours.'

'I need to see a man about a reindeer,' said Erkki, and started crawling out of the sleeping bag. The process was quick; he'd been sleeping with his leather winter boots on. He sat up in the middle of the back seat and expelled the air from his bowels, making a long, drumming sound against the fake leather seating, then got out of the car and closed the door behind him. Revenge for hitting him. And at the same time, an indication of just how much Erkki thought their mission, and, perhaps, the cause as a whole, stunk. Anneli had already had her doubts about how seriously he was taking all this, and the smell of rotten whale spreading through the car only seemed to confirm them. The harder question was what to do with a possible traitor.

Anneli returned the binoculars to her eyes.

There were two men. The Secretary had only mentioned one. Wait a minute – *Erkki* had only mentioned one man. Anneli didn't know what the Secretary had said. She placed the binoculars in her lap. Erkki returned to the car, sat down in the driver's seat, took a tub of sour yoghurt from the Spar bag at his feet. He opened the tub, took a spoon from his jacket pocket and began scooping up the frozen curds. Anneli watched as he popped one glob of yoghurt into his mouth at a time, let it melt, then swallowed it as if it were medicine. After finishing the yoghurt, Erkki bent down to the shopping bag again and pulled out a packet of frankfurters. He leant over, took a knife from the door's side compartment and slit the packet open. The sausages were frozen. Erkki cut one of them free and shoved it in his mouth to thaw. It stretched his cheeks. Anneli looked away and raised the binoculars to her eyes once more.

'Has the Secretary said anything about what happens next?' she asked.

The sounds of Erkki sucking on the half-frozen frankfurter stopped. 'Next?' he asked.

'Yes. Surely our work won't be done? The sofa will be in

Helsinki before the evening news. The revolution moves on apace, but Leningrad wasn't built in a day. What happens next?'

Erkki didn't answer right away.

'The work,' he said stiffly, 'will surely continue.'

'What kind of answer is that? How will it continue?'

Again, Anneli lowered her binoculars. There was nothing happening outside the house, nobody in sight. Erkki had thawed the sausage, and Anneli watched his Adam's apple as the wiener slid down his gullet.

'At the end of the day,' said Erkki, 'it depends on everything else, I suppose. This job. Life. Everything.'

Anneli looked at him more closely, tried to see whether his brain might have frozen while he was asleep or whether this restlessness was yet another sign that Erkki was no longer one of them.

'Do you mean your own life?'

Erkki looked down at the packet of sausages. 'What else is life?' he asked. 'If not each individual's, each creature's, each organism's and spore's own life?'

Yes, thought Anneli. Erkki's brain really had frozen stiff.

'Soon you'll be saying you believe in individualism,' she said. 'That each person should be able to make their own decisions and to hell with the common good. You're dangerously close to it.'

Erkki said nothing. He cut off another sausage and popped it in his mouth, sideways. His frosty cheeks bulged.

'We are working for the future,' said Anneli. 'For the good of the generations to come. That's what our lives are for. And everything's at stake. If we don't make sacrifices and if we don't win, there will be nobody here to defend civilisation and peace and what is right. Surely that's not what you want.'

Erkki said something, but Anneli couldn't make out what. The horizontal frankfurter must have been blocking his tongue. It didn't matter. Anneli hadn't finished.

'It seems to me that you've started to get all kinds of subversive thoughts into your head,' she said. 'And thoughts like that are the root of all evil. That's why you shouldn't think them at all. For the common good. We should guard our own thinking just as we guard other people's.'

The sausage snapped in two, and Erkki could speak again.

'Any movement outside the house?' he asked.

Anneli realised that Erkki was changing the subject, but there was a reason for this. She aimed the binoculars at the house and saw the same mammoth beast that had stopped them making any progress the previous night. She saw the light-blue van but no people. Until now, she had counted a total of three people in the garden, and she sincerely hoped that they wouldn't gain one or more extra passengers with each successive pitstop. She handed Erkki the binoculars, said she needed some air.

Anneli stepped out of the car, trudged through the snow to the edge of the woods and, after walking for a few minutes, decided she was sufficiently hidden among the spruces. With her felt boots, she dug a little hole in the snow over which she could crouch. She pulled down her padded winter trousers, hearing the squawk of the crows further off. The freezing air gripped her buttocks and private parts, but she felt a great sense of relief. She had been awake most of the night, and had stayed in the car to keep an eye on the house while Erkki snored and spluttered and moaned like a baby that had reached retirement age. She squeezed out the last drops into the eastern-Finnish wilderness, stood up, pulled up her trousers, tucked in the layers of vests and undershirts, and was about to go back to the car when she saw other footprints in the snow. Or, not the prints themselves, but a reflection, a glare next to them...

Erkki had done his business in almost exactly the same spot, about twenty metres away.

Anneli waded through the snow to the spot where Erkki had answered the call of nature. The smell was familiar from the car, the heap of dark-brown waste made her think of the bears living in the area. But it wasn't this that had caught her attention. The shiny brochure beside the heap must have fallen from Erkki's pocket – either that or he had abandoned it after a little reading session in the frozen woods. Anneli had reason to suspect the former: she recognised the name and logo on the front. A respected, traditional, high-quality auction house specialising in antiques. Anneli picked up the brochure, looked at it, opened it. Page after page of the distasteful, old-fashioned status symbols of the bourgeoisie, yes, but some pretty chests of drawers, vases, mirrors – and sofas. She looked at the starting prices and knew that they were just that: starting prices. She folded the brochure back to its original size and slipped it into the pocket of her winter jacket. She knew that the brochure meant something. Erkki hadn't shown it to her, hadn't mentioned it – on the contrary, he had assured her that he didn't care what happened to the sofa once they had delivered it. This new discovery suggested that simply wasn't true.

She heard Erkki starting the engine.

10

Ilmari stepped out into the garden carrying a cardboard box, and his aunt followed him. The morning was still nothing more than a faint violet-orange glimmer far to the east. Their breath steamed in the cold, the snow crunched underfoot, the air was still, and the world seemed to extend no further than the yard and the forest surrounding it.

'I packed food that will last,' said his aunt. 'I think anything would last, frankly. I doubt there's much in the way of heating in the back of that van.'

Ilmari didn't mention that there were other problems when it came to keeping the Thames warm. He untied the strings holding the back doors together, managed to open them and placed the box of food next to the sofa. He straightened his back, turned and knew exactly what his aunt was going to say.

'It's even more beautiful than I'd imagined,' she said. 'No wonder somebody wants to get their hands on it.'

Ilmari looked from his aunt to the sofa he was delivering. He thought about the events and emotions of the previous day. His aunt surely hadn't intended her words as a warning, but Ilmari noticed that they touched a nerve within him, a nerve that seemed constantly on guard. He closed the doors and started retying the strings.

'Whoever it is,' he said as he worked, 'they'll get the sofa in Kilpisjärvi, just as I promised.'

His aunt didn't answer straight away.

'I just can't help myself,' she said eventually.

'What do you mean?'

'Fretting about you.'

'As I said last night, there's no need to—'

'I still see that same little boy,' she said. 'The boy who wouldn't trust anybody.'

Ilmari finally managed to tie the doors closed, then glanced up at the house. He couldn't see Antero anywhere. Presumably he still hadn't finished his breakfast. How many eggs could fit into such a slender man?

'If it's my divorce you're worried about,' Ilmari began, 'it was all very amicable. Tuuli and I are still on good terms.'

'Of course you are,' said his aunt. 'At least, you *think* you're on good terms. You're a safe distance away now where no one can hurt you – or touch you for that matter. And where you don't have to trust anybody.'

Ilmari said nothing.

'But is that the meaning of life, the point of this existence, to put yourself on the outside and keep everything else a sharp spear's length away?'

Ilmari looked at the wooden, red-painted house and tried to remember how many years his aunt had lived here. Nine, maybe ten already?

'You moved here from Helsinki,' he said. 'You live alone with only the bears and wolves for company. Isn't that just another way of keeping life at arm's length?'

'I wasn't talking about geographical distance,' she said, and following his gaze, and they both stood looking at her house. 'But you might be right. Maybe I should pay more attention to my own sermons.'

Ilmari instantly regretted what he'd said. The last thing he wanted to do was upset or offend his aunt.

'I didn't mean—'

'You're important to me, Ilmari,' she said, not sounding at all offended. 'You know how things turned out with my family and, by extension, your family. If we leave out the drunks, the real drunks and all the other lost souls, there's only a few of us left. You and me, and your daughter, of course.'

'I know.'

His aunt nodded towards the house. More specifically, the kitchen window. 'You could let someone in there get a little closer, you know,' she said.

Ilmari looked at his aunt.

'No offence,' he said, 'but we're not about to get married. He's a mechanic.'

Ilmari's aunt shook her head. 'He might be a mechanic, but perhaps he's someone you can trust.'

Ilmari was about to ask how his aunt had reached that conclusion when Antero finally appeared. He sat himself on the frozen railing and slid down into the garden in style, all with perfect balance, as though he had done it a thousand times. Still, once on the ground he did walk rather stiffly, which Ilmari thought must have been due to the morning cold and their physical exertion the night before.

'I ate the ham,' said Antero once he reached the van. 'And finished off the pancakes too. And the jam, emptied the jar. I haven't eaten this well in years. I mean it. Thank you.'

'Thank you for cutting down that tree,' said Ilmari's aunt. 'I've packed some food for the road.'

'If only I could make it up to you,' said Antero.

'Perhaps you'll have the opportunity one day,' she replied.

Antero's eyes appeared fixed on Ilmari's aunt's. 'I'll try to make sure that happens.'

'Just try to take care of Ilmari,' replied his aunt.

'That's exactly what I meant,' Antero nodded.

Ilmari wasn't sure what to think about what they were saying, and, particularly, *how* they were saying it. As though Antero and his aunt had known each other before and this wasn't their first encounter but a long-awaited reunion. Then Antero spun around and disappeared behind the van. Ilmari heard the doors opening, a clatter, then the sound of the doors closing again. Ilmari gave his aunt a hug, got into the van and felt a great wave of emotion, which he tried to swallow. He reversed in front of the outbuilding, turned the van and drove down to the road.

Morning began to break, the crusted snow glistening where the rising sun shone between the trees. As they drove, Antero slipped a tape into the machine, and a moment later Blondie's 'The Tide Is High' filled the cab. Ilmari noted which tape Antero had selected: this too was one of his mix tapes. Maybe Antero thought it fitted the morning mood. Ilmari decided to listen to a few songs before asking.

Ilmari informed Antero that once they reached the main highway they would continue through Ilomantsi and would not stop for petrol until they were about to pass Kuopio. Antero thought this a sensible plan.

The road ran through the forest, the snow piled high on both sides, and there were no cars coming in the opposite direction. One song ended, another began, and Ilmari recognised this one too. He had listened to the album it came from in the record shop at the station when it had first come out about a month ago and liked what he had heard. 'Russian Roulette' by The Lords of the New Church began with the chattering of a helicopter's blades. They reached a sharp bend in the road, and Ilmari instinctively slowed more than was necessary. At first he didn't know quite know where this instinct had come from, but a moment later he realised.

An egg-yolk-yellow Lada was sitting sideways across the road, blocking the way.

Ilmari slammed his foot on the brake pedal as though he were trying to press it through the floor. The Thames slid, turned, slid, turned. Ilmari managed to correct their course, and eventually the Thames straightened up and came to a halt.

There was a metre between the Thames and the Lada.

A very short metre, thought Ilmari.

The bonnet of the egg-yolk-yellow Lada was standing upright, the driver's door was open. Ilmari saw an elderly man crouched over the engine – his clothes suggesting that he had appeared in the frozen morning straight out of the 1950s. Ilmari's first thought was the obvious one: the elderly driver made a simple driving mistake, and as a result his Lada had struck the embankment and stalled. Ilmari was about to say this out loud when two observations stopped him in his tracks.

Firstly, blue-grey smoke was billowing from the Lada's exhaust pipe. Which meant that the engine was running and there was nothing wrong with the car that would have forced it to come to a stop sideways across the road. His second observation – which he made in the Thames's wing mirror – was even more surprising. In the mirror, Ilmari saw a figure dressed in black trousers, a red jacket and a black balaclava – with a pistol. The figure was approaching from the left.

'There's someone on my side of the van,' he said to Antero, 'with a gun.'

'It's an ambush,' said Antero. 'The van will shield me. I'll move the Lada. Pick me up on the other side. They won't shoot their own car.'

Ilmari then witnessed a very brief piece of theatre.

Antero slipped out of the van, left the door open, took a few steps, sat in the already running Lada, put it in gear and pressed the accelerator. The Lada leapt forwards, and the old man, who was still hidden behind the bonnet, was shoved backwards, flying off the road and out of sight into the ditch. Antero then slid out of the Lada via the passenger door, used the car as a screen while he moved back to his side of the van. At the same time, Ilmari moved the van between the boot of the Lada and the verge, where Antero seamlessly slipped back into the Thames.

As Ilmari hit the accelerator, he looked in the wing mirror and saw the armed figure trying to reach the Lada. He saw the figure raise the gun and aim it at the van, but he didn't hear any shots, though they might have been drowned out by the roar of the Thames's engine and the climax of 'Russian Roulette'. They reached the next bend in the road, and the Lada disappeared from the wing mirror. They would soon be in Ilomantsi, thought Ilmari, and there they would either find a policeman or the police would find them.

'I didn't get the Lada into the ditch,' said Antero, almost apologetically. 'They'll be after us.'

11

The Finnish winter was like a terrible bout of diarrhoea: it ripped open your head and your arse all at once. After a frozen, sleepless night, Otto Puolanka was going about his morning business when he suddenly noticed flashes of light blue among the black and white of the birches, and immediately realised what he was seeing. He poured the dregs of his bottle of beer into his mouth, gargled and swallowed, then pushed his toothbrush into the pocket of his leather jacket. He threw the empty bottle into the snow, dashed to the car and congratulated himself for having kept the engine running. He congratulated himself for another thing too: he had chosen an excellent vantage point. He had correctly read the map he'd stolen from the petrol station the previous night. This was the route that the little devil transporting the sofa would choose if he really was on his way to Vaasa, as the junk merchant, who'd died of his own stupidity, had told him.

And now that van had just driven past him. Catching up with it would be a piece of cake, he thought. The Saab 96 was made for situations like this, which required both speed and agility. Besides, there was only one route the van could take on its way to Joensuu and from there to Kuopio and finally to Vaasa. So Otto knew exactly where the van was going.

He pulled onto the road and was about to speed off after the van when his right foot instinctively eased off the accelerator and then slammed on the brake.

An egg-yolk-yellow Lada scraped the front of the Saab's bonnet.

He had no idea where the Lada could have come from. It was travelling fast, as fast as a Lada could go. He shouted out loud, cursed all the bad drivers of the world, looked left and realised that he hadn't looked that way before. He couldn't see anyone or anything. His rage grew even more. He pressed the accelerator. The Saab was warm and excitable.

Otto switched on the tape player. He had rewound the tape to exactly the right place for a situation just like this. The opening riff of 'Eye of the Tiger' gave him a familiar rush of adrenaline. He imagined Rocky boxing, imagined him practising, really practising, sparring with Apollo Creed. He saw Mr T practising, alone, bursting with anger. Otto understood Mr T. But he understood Sylvester Stallone even more, and he was sure that, if he and Stallone ever met, they would have plenty in common. Rambo was evidence of that. Otto nodded his head in time with the music, the Saab gobbled up the road, and the Finnish winter landscape, gleaming in the morning sunshine, flew past on both sides.

By the time Otto finally caught sight of the van again, he couldn't remember how many times he had wound the tape back to the beginning and listened to 'Eye of the Tiger'. He wanted the song to be playing at the very moment he got the better of the van driver and told him exactly what he thought about being taken on a wild-goose chase in this infernal cold.

But it wasn't just the van that he saw. He saw the egg-yolk-yellow Lada too and the doddery old fart who had almost crashed into him. What the hell is this? Otto wondered. The Lada was on the van's tail. Both vehicles looked like they were being pushed to the limit, and both were driving right down the middle of the highway. They looked almost glued together, and snow was billowing behind them, but they were far enough ahead that it didn't affect Otto.

Then, just as he caught up with the van and the Lada, the song on the tape changed. It was The Pointer Sisters' 'I'm So Excited', or so he had read on the back of the cassette. Otto knew very well what it meant to be excited. Right now, he was very excited. 'I'm about to lose control, and I think I like it.'

The panorama opened up, the road stretched out ahead of them. Otto was about to choose between a number of options – he could certainly overtake the Lada, and maybe even the van too, and maybe force both of them to stop, and at the same time teach the Lada driver a thing or two about the highway code – when he saw something that made him reassess his plans.

The van jolted, swerved towards the hard shoulder. The Lada took this opportunity to drive right up next to the van, but it didn't even try to overtake. The two vehicles were now driving side by side, the Lada facing the oncoming traffic. Otto was certain that both vehicles had reached their maximum speed.

And only a second later, Otto saw something even more astonishing.

The Lada's passenger window opened.

The sleeve of a winter jacket appeared from the window.

And at the end of that sleeve was a pistol.

12

They were driving far too fast, and the Thames was showing signs of overheating. Ilmari had managed to keep the Lada behind him, but he realised that this alone didn't solve their immediate problem: if the Lada remained where it was, they wouldn't be able to shake it off. With this in mind, as the road stretched out ahead of them, Ilmari steered the car tight against the hard shoulder, allowing the Lada to move up alongside them.

And it was then that they saw the pistol.

'If they shoot,' said Antero, 'I hope they aim for the cab.'

'What?' asked Ilmari.

'The tyres are more vulnerable,' said Antero.

Ilmari had to admit that Antero was right. They had to keep the van roadworthy, come what may. Besides, it looked as though Antero's wish was about to come true. The pistol was aimed right at Ilmari.

Now Ilmari finally got a good look at the person holding the pistol. He saw a black balaclava, long, thick brown hair flowing from beneath it, fluttering against a red puffer jacket. From the opening in the front of the balaclava, he saw a mouth frantically forming words. He couldn't make them out, but their message was clear. Ilmari had no intention of heeding their command.

After speeding along the long, straight stretch of road for a while, Ilmari spotted a gentle bend up ahead. The road curved to the right and disappeared somewhere behind the wall of trees. And it was then that the idea began to take shape in his mind.

There were no other options. The roads and town were deserted, so there was no point waiting for the police to rush to their aid. The person brandishing the gun seemed more than a little unstable and could explode at any moment. And Ilmari didn't want to end up in a situation whereby he had to give up the sofa. (The sofa was tantamount to his daughter's piano. He would not give it up.)

He made up his mind and told Antero to hold on tight.

Time for the bend.

The Lada was alongside them, the mouth of the pistol almost touching the van. Ilmari didn't know how long the person still bellowing at them would refrain from pulling the trigger. They were almost at the end of the straight section, and if he were properly following the bend in the road, Ilmari should already have started gently turning the steering wheel. But he did not. The difference between the curve of the road and the van's course was a matter of only a few degrees, but their speed only increased the effect of his chosen trajectory. Both vehicles began veering to the left, and a moment later the Lada's left-hand side scuffed against the verge. Now Ilmari concluded that the Lada was driving at top speed too. And now, as the amount of available road became smaller by the millisecond, all it could do was give up or fall behind them or...

The Lada's driver made his decision. The shove was doomed to failure. Though the Thames was old and small for a van, it was still considerably heavier than the Lada. And the Lada had no room for manoeuvre on the other side. The Lada gently tapped the Thames, bounced back in the other direction and struck the piled snow along the left-hand verge with far greater power than it had the Thames. One touch was enough. The Lada disappeared from alongside the van. Ilmari looked in the wing mirror, saw the Lada swerving, spinning and eventually disappearing in an enormous cloud of snow.

Ilmari brought the Thames back to the right-hand side of the road and slowed up. The engine had to cool down.

'Nice move,' said Antero.

'It was all I could think of,' said Ilmari. And it was true.

'Sometimes one option is enough,' said Antero.

They drove for a long while without seeing anyone. Ilmari didn't feel the need to speak. He wanted to think.

'I don't mean to spoil the atmosphere,' said Antero after a while, 'but I think there was another car on our tail too – a dark-green Saab 96.'

Ilmari looked in the wing mirror. All he could see was the forest and the road.

'I can't see it,' he said.

'Neither can I,' said Antero. 'And I haven't seen it for some time. But I'm quite sure it was there.'

Ilmari returned to his thoughts. He didn't like where they led him.

'Keep an eye on the mirror,' he said. 'If the Saab appears, we'll think of something.'

They drove through Joensuu, crossed the river. Under different circumstances, Ilmari would have stopped in the town shrouded in winter frost for a tasty Vyborg pretzel and a cup of coffee. And given what he now knew about Antero, he was sure he wouldn't have turned his nose up at the local delicacies, or any other delicacies for that matter. But something was off kilter. Ilmari thought through everything that he could recall from the last twenty-four hours. Twenty minutes later, he asked Antero if he had seen the Saab. Antero said he hadn't seen hide nor tail of it.

Ilmari saw a small road coming up ahead. He turned onto it and drove for another few minutes. Spotting the end of a ploughed forest road, he pulled over into the protection of the trees and drove very slowly for another fifty metres along the track, before stopping the car and switching off the engine. He got out of the van, smelt the cold forest and felt the silence around them. He walked round to the back of the van. Antero appeared next to him as he untied the string holding the doors together. Ilmari opened one door, Antero the other.

They saw exactly what they were expecting to see: a magnificent antique sofa.

Ilmari had never heard of an armed robbery over a sofa. In all the years he'd been actively frequenting the cinema, how many films had he seen about sofa heists? Exactly. But neither did he believe this was about drugs, for instance, because as he and Antero had noted, they were travelling in the wrong direction to be transporting drugs. And yet, someone was prepared to set traps and point a gun at them, to race them along the highway and try to run them off the road. All for a sofa.

Ilmari removed the ropes holding the sofa in place, jumped into the back of the van, squeezed in behind the sofa and asked Antero to grip the other end. The first thing they noticed was how heavy the sofa was. It weighed more than it should have. After much sweating and searching for the best way to lift it, they finally managed to get the sofa out of the van and onto the forest road. The sunlight filtering between the trees accentuated its generous form, the blood-red of the upholstery, the beauty of the smooth, carved dark-wood finishings.

Ilmari walked around the sofa first once, then twice. And stood behind it.

Oddly, the upholstery on the back of the sofa was in two parts. Ilmari had never seen anything like this before and didn't think it a very usual solution. The lower part of the upholstery was the height of a chair and the width of the sofa, as was the upper part. The beams of sunlight pushing their way between the birches struck the sofa at just the right angle, highlighting how the lower part of the sofa was slightly raised and stuck out a fraction more than the larger, upper part. As though the upholstery and the entire lower part of the sofa were under some kind of strain from the inside. The more closely Ilmari examined the lower part of the sofa, the more certain he was that this was not a deliberate bulge or protuberance. Something was pushing the two parts of the sofa apart.

He asked Antero to grip one end of the lower part of the sofa and to pull when he gave the word. He took hold of the sofa, and Antero nodded. The lower section moved. Ilmari said *now*, and they wrenched it harder. The lower part of the sofa came off completely and fell into the snow. Ilmari and Antero jumped backwards.

They both stood staring at the hand dangling from inside the sofa.

13

Ilmari wasn't sure how long they stood there in the silent, gleaming forest, staring at the thick fingers, the pallid wrist, the forearm covered in dark hair protruding from the blood-red antique sofa. At some point, Ilmari found himself thinking about the last song he had heard in the van. Irene Cara's 'Fame' felt like a prediction of what was in front of them, and not in the best way.

The arm remained still; Ilmari hadn't expected anything else. He had seen his grandfather's body a few years ago and knew what the dead looked like. They didn't try to climb out of their sofas; they stayed firmly put. Whoever was in this sofa was very certainly dead and almost certainly a man: every visible part of him was bruised, broad and hairy. There were even hairs on his fingers. Ilmari looked up at the surrounding trees, then further up still. The blue canopy of the sky extended in all directions. He thought carefully, then spoke.

'Let's lift this back into the van,' he said. 'Then we'll call the police.'

He looked down again and was about to take a step towards the piece of the sofa that had fallen into the snow when he noticed that Antero was still staring at the hand. He didn't look particularly shocked, but more like he was pondering something.

'The police?' he asked. 'Are you sure?'

'I don't know what else we can do,' said Ilmari. 'There's somebody in that sofa. We're shipping a dead man around Finland in an old van. I don't know about you, but I think this is quite an unexpected and ... unusual turn of events.'

'That's what I mean,' said Antero. 'Everything that's happened this morning is unusual. First the ambush, then the Keijo Rosberg Formula One stunt a minute ago. The gun. Maybe the Saab too.'

Ilmari had thought the same things and didn't like where his thoughts had taken him. He gave a sigh.

'I've never met the guy who gave me this job,' he said, as much to himself as to Antero. 'We just talked on the telephone. I picked up the van and the sofa at the designated location. But I never met him in person. Which means, I wouldn't be able to identify him in a line-up. I have no idea who we're dealing with.'

'And you still want to go to the police?' asked Antero.

Ilmari knew what he was getting at.

'Getting the police involved isn't ideal,' he said, and then more to himself than to Antero: 'But I don't know what else to do. Let's get this sofa back in the van, then I'll make some calls. First to my contact. Then the police.'

Neither of them were especially keen to touch the hand. Eventually, they raised the lower part of the sofa and the hand seemed to return inside the sofa of its own accord. They managed to reattach the lower section by manually pushing the nails back in their holes. Neither of them had to say out loud that the lower section was only loosely held in place and would detach again very easily. Right now, that didn't feel like the biggest of their problems.

They drove back down the track and returned to the forest road, keeping watch in the wing mirrors, but they couldn't see any signs of the egg-yolk-yellow Lada or the dark-green Saab 96. All the same, they decided not to stop until they reached Tuusniemi, just in case. And once there Ilmari parked the van behind the service station so it couldn't be seen from the highway. Both precautions felt necessary.

Ilmari counted his coins before getting back in the car. He had enough marks for several long-distance calls. He hoped this would be enough.

'I don't think our guy's going anywhere,' said Antero, 'but maybe best if I keep watch.'

Ilmari agreed. The ad hoc string lock on the back doors felt a little flimsier now that they knew exactly what they were transporting. Ilmari walked into the service station, saw the locals in their thick winter clothes in the cosy cafeteria with its low ceilings and birch panelling, and found a public telephone by the toilets. He took a scrap of paper from his jacket pocket, held the receiver to his ear, dropped a coin in the slot and dialled first zero nine, the code for Helsinki, then the rest of the numbers, one at a time. The telephone rang only once. Ilmari didn't recognise the voice that answered. He introduced himself, said that he had recently taken on a delivery job and had just realised that there was more to this particular piece of furniture than met the eye.

'I know who you are,' said the voice. 'And I know what you're talking about.'

'Good,' said Ilmari. 'Because I don't.'

'Where are you calling from?' asked the voice.

Ilmari didn't plan to give his precise location. That had been one of the problems with this journey: so many people seemed to know exactly where he was and when. Ilmari said nothing.

'I understand,' said the voice. 'You haven't been in touch with anyone else, have you? Other ... operators?'

'You mean the police?' asked Ilmari.

'It's extremely important that this remains between us.'

'But it *hasn't* remained between us, has it?'

Silence.

'Yeah,' said the voice. 'Sorry about that. Our organisation has a leak.'

'A leak?'

'That has now been located and ... neutralised, shall we say. But the damage has already been done, and the people who shouldn't have known about this have now found out about it. And there's more bad news, too.'

'How much worse could it possibly get?' asked Ilmari.

'I'll be straight with you,' said the voice.

'I think that would be for the best,' said Ilmari.

'If you talk to the police,' the voice began, and Ilmari noted how it was now a little lower in both pitch and temperature, 'you'll be next in the sofa.'

Ilmari didn't answer at first.

'That is bad news,' he agreed after a beat.

'And if the sofa doesn't get to Kilpisjärvi,' the voice continued, cooling even further, 'you'll be next in the sofa.'

'That's bad news too,' Ilmari agreed for a second time.

'It's important that you understand this.'

'I've seen what's in the sofa.'

'Good,' said the voice, which by now sounded – if possible – a little more relaxed. 'Thanks for calling. I appreciate it.'

Ilmari dropped another mark into the slot. The coin disappeared into the machine, and the telephone gave a crackle.

'Who is he?' asked Ilmari.

The voice didn't respond immediately. Then: 'Have you heard of Matti Vanamo?'

Of course Ilmari had heard of Matti Vanamo. Everybody had heard of Matti Vanamo. Synonymous with the Helsinki criminal underworld, his name was even used to refer to any boss or leader, and not always in a positive way. Ilmari admitted that he knew who Vanamo was.

'Well, now you've met him in the flesh,' said the voice.

Ilmari thought it best not to say that he had almost shaken hands with Vanamo.

'Why is he in the sofa?' he asked.

'The more you know,' said the voice, 'the more dangerous it will be for you.'

'Not knowing anything feels pretty dangerous too,' said Ilmari.

'Fine,' the voice conceded. 'Let me put it this way: the manner of his death might interest our competitors. A lot. Or rather, if the manner of his death were to become public, it would hurt us. A lot. An autopsy in Helsinki would bring everything to light. That's why we need to get the body first to Kilpisjärvi, then smuggled out of the country.'

Ilmari picked up a third mark. 'Who knows that I'm transporting this sofa?'

'To be honest,' said the voice, dragging out the answer so much that Ilmari could imagine the owner of the voice staring out across a panorama without finding anything to latch on to, 'all the wrong people and organisations.'

Ilmari was silent for a moment.

'Why am I transporting the sofa?' he asked.

'Because you were completely unknown and completely outside our circles,' said the voice. 'Nobody was supposed to know anything about you. And when you told us about your route, which isn't exactly the most direct or logical one, you were the perfect choice. Speaking of the route, I still think it's the best solution.'

'Even though everybody knows about it?'

'Everybody knows about Kilpisjärvi,' said the voice. 'But nobody knows exactly when you're going to be there so, in a sense, time is on your side.'

Ilmari didn't mention that he planned to be at the instrument store on Aleksanterinkatu before midday on Christmas Eve. In that sense, time wasn't really on his side at all. He dropped the third mark into the telephone.

'What about these organisations,' he asked, 'these people that are after me?'

'I think some of them might be armed.'

'There's no might about it,' said Ilmari. 'I can confirm they are definitely armed.'

'That's too bad,' said the voice. 'Makes things a bit riskier...'

'Who are they?'

'As far as I know, it's quite a motley crew,' said the voice. 'At least one of the groups is planning a Marxist-Leninist revolution, then there's a guy we know who's doing a bit of freelancing. We try to avoid him. Because we know him.'

'You...' Ilmari began, 'try to avoid him?'

'We've decided he's too unpredictable, too dangerous.'

Ilmari said nothing.

'Not to put too fine a point on it,' the voice continued, 'but at this stage I think it's safe to say that if any of them tracks you down, they will take you out.'

Ilmari took a deep breath. In just a short space of time, he had been given – he counted them – three different scenarios of how he might end up dead because of this sofa.

'One more question,' he said.

'I imagine this is about you?'

'Yes,' said Ilmari. 'How do I know I won't end up in the sofa or some other unfortunate place once I've delivered it?'

'Because we admire what you've done so far,' said the voice. 'And we won't forget it. We're known for keeping our word. We have promised you payment for delivering the sofa to Kilpisjärvi, and if you do it, if you safely deliver the sofa to our partner in Kilpisjärvi, we will pay you the agreed sum of money.'

'And that's it?'

'That's it,' said the voice, now sounding more genuine than at any time during the phone call. 'We don't have any demands other than those I've already spelled out.'

Ilmari put the fourth mark back in his pocket. He didn't want to continue this conversation. Not that there was any need to continue it. He knew the essentials. He thanked the voice for this new information, bid him a nice afternoon and replaced the receiver on its steel hook. He stood in front of the telephone a moment longer, then went to the toilet. Then he walked back out through the cafeteria and the locals wrapped up in puffer jackets and found Antero waiting next to the van. He told him about the phone call. Antero tousled his already tousled hair. He looked pensive. Then he gave a nod.

'Good to know,' he said.

14

Sparsely populated areas were like parts of the body suffering from an advanced sexually transmitted disease: all sensation had died long ago. Otto Puolanka knew – because he'd heard it in prison – that country folk didn't just milk their cows. A shudder ran through him as he marched along the side of the road in the freezing cold. But though the feeling was powerful, it wasn't as visceral as the anger bubbling inside him.

The fact that his car had run out of petrol at the crucial moment was, from Otto's perspective, not his own fault; it was the fault of the guy he was chasing. And neither was it Otto's fault that the Finnish winter had forced him to keep the engine idling almost right through the night. And now, because of all the above, he found himself having to walk back the way he had come to the service station he had seen a moment earlier while he had been following the light-blue van.

Otto knew for a fact what the light-blue van contained. He wasn't quite so sure about the egg-yolk-yellow Lada that had run into the ditch. The Lada had been following the Thames, just like him. As he had passed the Lada, he had seen two people inside. He wasn't surprised that there was someone else after the sofa besides him. That happened in situations like this. It just meant he would have to take out a few more people along the way. It was a cold day, but Otto hadn't zipped up his jacket and instead let the two sides flutter.

Eventually, the service station appeared – it seemed to leap out at him from behind the trees. One moment it was hidden behind the woods, and the next Otto was walking into its forecourt.

Once inside the service station shop, he walked directly to a small hardware section, bought a plastic canister and three packets of Camels, and walked out to the pumps. He filled the canister, breathed in the pleasant aroma of petrol, closed the canister, left it next to the pump and went back inside to pay. The assistant, a dark-haired woman in heavy make-up, asked Otto if he wanted anything else, from the café, maybe. Of course not, you stupid cow, do I look like I come to dumps like this for fun, he was about to say, but at just that moment he happened to look out at the road. The cold seemed to vanish from him, he could feel his whole body suddenly warming, right down to his fingertips, really heating up.

Otto saw the egg-yolk-yellow Lada pulling up on the forecourt, with some difficulty. Even from indoors, he could hear there was something wrong with the engine – the sound was high-pitched and uneven. Crashing into a ditch will do that. The Lada drove past the shop and café and continued to the repair workshop at the back of the building. Otto looked around, then turned to the assistant.

'I'll take a shovel,' he said. 'And a cup of coffee.'

He carried his cup of steaming coffee and his brand-new steel tool to a table, sat down, and realised that he was the only customer in the café. He placed the shovel next to him, where he would be able to grab hold of it quickly, if necessary, and waited. He sipped his coffee and was taken aback. He liked bitter coffee, but this tasted like it had been mixed with a pot of burnt plastic. He lit a cigarette and continued waiting. A red Datsun curved onto the forecourt; a man in his sixties stepped out of the car, walked inside and headed straight for the toilet. A moment passed, the man came out of the toilet and stopped for a chat with the assistant. All part of the same incestuous bunch, thought Otto.

Then he saw something he had hoped he would see before long: one of the passengers from the Lada.

This man was in his sixties too, but that was where the similarities with the Datsun driver ended. This man looked like a rock of granite that had grown legs and started walking. His grey hair gleamed like a silver helmet in the horizontal winter sunlight, and he limped on his right leg, which suggested to Otto that the man must have hurt it quite badly, though his stony face revealed not even one flicker of pain or discomfort. The man stepped inside, and he too headed straight for the toilet, without looking towards the café. Otto waited a second, another, then stubbed out his cigarette. He picked up the shovel, gripped it in his right hand, stood up and stepped quickly over to the toilet door, and just as he reached his left hand towards the handle, the door opened.

Otto changed direction at the last minute. He returned to the small hardware section where he had begun, just as the granite man stepped out of the toilet and walked towards the front door. Otto thought he might be on his way back outside, but he stopped at a telephone booth by the door. The man rummaged in his pocket for a coin, found one, and dialled a number. While he was waiting for an answer, his eyes flicked around the room, checking the counter and the café area. But it seemed he hadn't spotted Otto, who was now standing just two metres behind him.

'It's me,' the man said into the telephone. 'All fine ... I just called to say everything's fine ... Yes, I'm sure ... just bashed my leg a bit ... Nothing serious ... I was changing the tyre and twisted my knee ... No, no, the car's just great, runs like a dream ... I just called to say this is going to take a while ... An unexpected detour to Vaasa, and from there to Helsinki ... The exact address ... Sahaluodonkatu ... It's quick and easy ... yes ... I promise ... There won't be any problems...'

The man ended the call, turned again and went back into the toilet. Again, Otto waited a second, another, and was about to follow the man and his silver helmet of hair, but then the Datsun driver, who had been talking to the sales assistant, suddenly decided that he needed the toilet again. Otto felt a deep sense of frustration, but what could he do about old men's prostates? Loose plumbing starts to become a bit of a problem. He would have to come up with something else.

He pulled on his gloves, picked up his shovel and left the shop. He walked around the building, saw the Lada and was taken aback for a second time. A woman of about thirty was busying herself at the back of the car, looking for something in the boot. She noticed Otto and stood up straight. Otto looked at her. Long, dark-brown hair, blue-green eyes and a red puffer jacket. Otto had seen the sleeve of that jacket before. He looked at her hand. This time, she wasn't brandishing a pistol.

'I think someone's having a medical emergency inside,' he said.

'Excuse me?'

'Your dad,' said Otto.

The penny seemed to drop. The woman shook her head. 'He's not my dad,' she said.

Interesting, thought Otto.

'Fainted,' he said. 'In the toilet.'

'What?'

'Looks pretty bad,' he said. 'With all the frothing at the mouth, I'd say it's rabies or something even worse.'

'Rabies...?'

Otto shrugged. 'I just hope the ambulance gets here in time,' he said. 'Big blisters on his face...'

The woman wasn't listening anymore. She had already shut the boot of the Lada and disappeared round the corner of the building.

Otto looked around. He couldn't see a mechanic anywhere, or anyone else. He opened the driver's door, unlocked the bonnet, closed the door, then lifted the Lada's bonnet. First, he pulled one of the leads free from the battery, hiding the end in among a tangle of other cables, then, using his shovel, he prised two large ports loose from the parts of the engine they belonged to. At first glance, everything looked just as it had done a moment earlier. That meant it would take some time to find the problem. Otto closed the bonnet and began walking the other way round the building. When he reached the corner at the front, he came to a stop.

He walked to the pump, moved the shovel into his left hand, picked up the canister with his right, and a moment later he was hidden among the trees.

15

What little was left of the day glowed up ahead. Gold was gathering along the horizon, a thin strip of violet running along its top. They were driving towards it. Ilmari Nieminen could still feel the adrenaline in his body, the sense of light and power that it bestowed upon him.

Ilmari didn't think he was going mad, though at this point it would have been perfectly understandable, but he felt he could now see things more clearly. He didn't know why this was happening at this particular moment, why being threatened with a pistol, his narrow escape and comprehending the full gravity of this lethal situation had made him suddenly recall many things, many events, that he hadn't thought about for years. And why did he now understand those events and his reactions to them with such clarity? He wasn't sure. But it had happened.

More surprising still, he felt the need to talk. At first, he couldn't explain why, but then he thought it was possibly the same phenomenon as when, years ago, he and another boy at the same summer job had found themselves in a situation in which they had to survive without the help of the full-time workers. The only way to get through the situation was by working together and trusting each other. Ilmari remembered that the experience had brought them closer together, and within the space of a single day a strong bond had formed between them. Something had made talking natural and, as extraordinary as it sounded to men like them, necessary too. And now – although they were childhood friends and, in that sense, they already knew each other – he and Antero had, in the space of a single morning, driven into an ambush, survived that ambush and the ensuing car chase, and found that they were transporting a dead man in a sofa, and their survival now depended on delivering both sofa and cadaver to the extreme north of Finland. That's more than a day's work at your average summer job.

Ilmari looked ahead, watched the highway, the darkening forest and the golden-violet horizon, and listened to the hum of the British four-stroke engine. He noted that neither of them had put a new tape in the cassette player. Ilmari was about to do so, when Antero broke the lengthy silence.

'The railway accident,' he began. 'The one I told you about. It wasn't an accident. I lay down on the tracks of my own accord. I was trying to top myself.'

Ilmari glanced to the side. Antero was staring at the road ahead. Ilmari couldn't know what was going through Antero's mind, but he thought it highly likely that Antero, like him, had been pondering the day's events.

'I wasn't at my best,' Antero continued. 'Which turned out to be a good thing. Drunkenness and a broken set of points meant that only my leg got crushed.'

Ilmari remained silent.

'I'd come back to Finland from the Foreign Legion,' said Antero. 'But I didn't fit in. Anywhere. I was what you might call a lone wolf.'

'But now,' said Ilmari, 'it seems you've turned things around?'

'Not really,' said Antero.

Ilmari waited for him to continue, but he didn't.

'I haven't got all that many friends either,' said Ilmari after a moment. 'Never did.'

'I know.'

'I haven't trusted anyone for a long, long time,' said Ilmari. 'Maybe I've never trusted anyone.'

'It's tough,' said Antero. 'A life like that.'

They drove on without speaking.

'I want to thank you for what you did this morning,' said Ilmari after four kilometres of silence. 'With the Lada.'

'That was an old trick,' said Antero. 'Nice to make myself useful.'

'Another thing,' said Ilmari. 'I'll understand if you want to jump ship at any point. Nobody knows about you. I made sure not to mention you on the phone.'

'I'm happy to stay.'

'It could be dangerous.'

'I know,' said Antero.

Again, they continued in silence.

'We might not have to be alone for much longer,' Ilmari said eventually. 'They might get the better of us before Vaasa.'

Ilmari glanced to the side, saw Antero's stern, serious face.

'That would certainly be an unfortunate turn of events,' he said. 'Seeing as this trip has got off to such a jolly start.'

The next silence lasted just half a second. Then they exploded. The laughter consumed them, filled the cab. Just then, a lorry loaded with logs shuddered past them, and for a long stretch afterwards they found themselves driving through the tunnel of snow left in the lorry's wake.

Once the landscape came back into view, Ilmari said: 'You haven't asked why we're going to Vaasa.'

'Why are we going to Vaasa?'

'To retrieve my leather jacket.'

Antero turned, and Ilmari was sure he could feel his companion's eyes on his right cheek.

'Your leather jacket?'

'My favourite jacket,' said Ilmari. 'Someone borrowed it from me. It was the last one in the shop, the last of its kind.'

For a moment, Antero remained silent, then he spoke.

'I'm not trying to be funny,' he said, 'but you are aware there's such a thing as the telephone and the post?'

'I work at the post office,' said Ilmari. 'And as you just saw, I know how to use a telephone. Every time I get hold of this guy, he has a different excuse. The post office had run out of stamps. He had the wrong address.'

'I understand,' said Antero. 'But how did someone like that get hold of your favourite jacket in the first place?'

Ilmari took a deep breath.

'It was at a Motörhead concert,' said Ilmari. 'At the Ice Stadium last November. I was there with some friends of friends, and one of them had come with an old mate from Vaasa. The band started playing 'Bomber', I was getting hot, so I took off my jacket and put it down. A moment later, I saw that this guy had put it on, said he was feeling cold and promised he'd give it back at the end of the gig. Okay, I said, and I've never seen him since. It's been over a year. I haven't got anything against him, or Vaasa. I just want my jacket back.'

'Does he know you're on your way?'

'Yes.'

'What did he sound like when you said you were coming to fetch your jacket?'

'Not very enthusiastic.'

Antero didn't answer and didn't say anything for a long time. Ilmari felt they had now had the conversation that needed to be had. Neither of them were particularly chatty people, and under the circumstances that too felt appropriate. But the fact of the matter was that they were still transporting a body, and a thing like that can't help but affect the general mood. When Antero finally did speak again, it was about music. Very quickly, they agreed that that was exactly what they needed. Almost immediately, Prince's '1999' filled the cab.

They continued driving towards Vaasa.

16

Anneli Kukkorinne looked again at Erkki Liljalampi, whose eyes were staring fixedly ahead. They were driving over the speed limit. Erkki's fingers, still black from fixing the engine, gripped the Lada's steering wheel. If his knuckles hadn't been covered in a thick layer of grime, thought Anneli, they would have been white as a sheet.

'Are you absolutely sure you didn't see the man at the service station?' she asked.

'I didn't see anyone who didn't belong there,' said Erkki. 'At any point.'

'What exactly did you do at the service station?'

'I went to the toilet, as you know fine well. You walked in on me at the urinal.'

Anneli looked at Erkki a moment longer, then turned her head. The road was taking them further into the dusk.

'He was a cowboy,' she said. 'Someone who thinks he's a cowboy. He was carrying that shovel the way people in Westerns carry a rifle. It was obvious mimicry. Propaganda and mass entertainment operate like that. People are more susceptible than ever to outside influence these days. I wouldn't be surprised if it turned out he was a fan of violent films.'

Erkki said nothing. He slipped a cigarette between his stony lips, lit it with the car's cigarette lighter. A moment later, the whole car smelt burnt.

'This means we've got competition,' Anneli continued. 'Other adversaries besides those goons in the van. Which means we have to get our hands on that sofa quicker than planned.'

Erkki continued staring at the road ahead and smoking his cigarette. Anneli hadn't forgotten the brochure she had found or Erkki's strange comments.

'Can I ask you something?' she asked.

'Sure,' said Erkki.

'How long have you known the Secretary?'

Erkki didn't reply right away.

'Decades, probably,' he said eventually.

'I assume he is unwavering when it comes to the cause?'

'Absolutely,' said Erkki, and sucked on his cigarette so vigorously that his head could have burst into flames.

'What about you?' asked Anneli.

Erkki coughed, perhaps because of the vigorous drag, or maybe for some other reason.

'I've been working to bring about the revolution for almost forty years,' he said.

Was that really an answer to Anneli's question? She didn't know. And how far could she push him? She needed Erkki, if only to complete this mission. She decided to shift focus.

'Why have I never been able to meet the Secretary?' she asked. 'At first I understood, but I've been involved in these missions for years now.'

'The less we—'

'The less we know about him,' Anneli completed the answer she had heard many times before, 'the safer it is for all concerned. Fine, I get it. But I'd just like to talk to him. Surely there's no danger in that? Could I have his phone number?'

Smoke rose from the cigarette between Erkki's fingers.

'With a number—'

'You can easily find out a name and address,' said Anneli. 'But if I call him at a specific time, in a specific place where he can answer safely, a café, a bar, something like that?'

'Why do you want to talk to him all of a sudden?' asked Erkki.

Because you are behaving so suspiciously, thought Anneli. Because I want to tell the Secretary about my observations. Just then, she noted a tiny change in Erkki's expression, which only very rarely changed at all. And in an instant, she realised something fundamental: now Erkki suspected *her*, suspected that she suspected him. Perhaps he even suspected that she suspected that he suspected she suspected him ... Anneli suddenly felt as though Erkki had led her into a trap. He was more experienced than her, that was true. What if Erkki and, by extension, the Secretary, doubted *her* dedication to the cause?

'It's not necessary,' she said quickly. 'I trust you and the Secretary and the cause. One hundred percent. I wasn't trying to cast doubt on anything. It was just ... small talk ... to pass the time.'

The smell of burning again filled the car. Erkki had lit another cigarette.

They continued driving towards Vaasa.

17

After arriving in Vaasa, Ilmari and Antero stopped at the Kesoil petrol station to fill up and ask for advice. They received instructions – this being Vaasa, in Swedish – to get them to their destination. The instructions were clear, and they arrived shortly before the evening news.

The house was within the city boundaries but was still out of the way. The post box by the road, which they used to check the right name and number, appeared lonely, no matter which way Ilmari looked at it. This felt like an area of the city that had been abandoned shortly after it was planned. There was no movement anywhere, but the junction where they had stopped was relatively large and designed to cope with a volume of traffic that in all likelihood would never materialise. The house stood right next to the road. An old red Citroën was parked outside the house, so Ilmari pulled the Thames up by the kerb and switched off the engine.

They got out of the van, took a few steps and remained standing on the spot for a moment. They looked in all possible directions, listened. Ilmari heard the occasional sound of traffic, acceleration, heavy lorries, cars, but all this was in the distance. Looking south, a halo of light hung above the town in the evening sky.

Ilmari looked at the red-brick house. It was only perhaps ten or fifteen years old, but it was in surprisingly bad shape. A building could only get into a condition like this through sustained, deliberate neglect. Almost everything that could come loose had come loose. Almost everything that could become

stained or waterlogged was stained and waterlogged. Someone
had clearly driven along the short driveway but not bothered to
plough the snow out of the way. The flat ceiling was weighed
down by a metre of snow, bowed and auguring future collapse.
Ilmari recalled that Salminen hadn't exactly given the impression
he was a hardworking man the last time they had met.

'The lights are on round the back,' said Antero.

Ilmari had noted this too. The windows facing the road were
dark, but the trees behind the house reflected a faint light coming
from inside. They stepped into the snow, walked between the
Citroën and the brick wall, went behind the house and saw the
illuminated window. They saw the kitchen and they saw a man
that Ilmari recognised as Salminen. He was doing something,
but the half curtain running along the bottom of the window
prevented them from seeing what. Salminen seemed both
hurried and focussed on whatever it was he was doing. They
waited a moment longer, then Ilmari took a few steps towards
the door and knocked. He stepped back a little, glanced into the
window. The kitchen was now empty. Then Salminen opened
the door.

Ilmari had expected Salminen to be either annoyed or at least
a little embarrassed at seeing him, but he was neither.

'The oven's on,' said Salminen. 'The rolls are just ready to go
in.'

Ilmari glanced at Antero, who looked back at him quizzically.
At least, that's how Ilmari interpreted Antero's expressionlessness
on this occasion.

'Ham and cheese,' Salminen continued. 'Warm ham and
cheese rolls.'

Salminen had fair hair and a ruddy complexion, and was
shaped like an average-sized antique column with his hair short
on top and at the sides and a generous mullet at the back. He was

wearing a KISS T-shirt, faded from a thousand washes and bearing the text *HOTTER THAN HELL*, worn-out jeans and, the icing on the cake, a pair of wooden shoes. He wasn't sporting Ilmari's leather jacket, but in all other respects he looked just as he had done at the concert a year ago. Before Ilmari could say anything, Salminen was already showing them indoors.

They left their outdoor shoes in the hallway, which smelt of animals, and stepped inside. The interior of the living room had met the same fate as the rest of the house. Ilmari couldn't help thinking that Salminen must either have inherited the house, furniture and all, or acquired it some other way and simply started living there without any other intention or need to change it. Ilmari and Antero sat down on a sofa behind a glass coffee table. Salminen pottered in the kitchen a while longer, opened the oven, slid the baking trays in, closed the oven door, then returned to the living room and sat down in an armchair next to the kitchen door.

'The rolls are in the oven,' he said.

'Thank you,' said Ilmari. 'That's nice.' He paused, then continued: 'As I said on the phone, we're on quite a tight schedule, so if I could just get my jacket...'

'Of course,' said Salminen, and again disappeared from the living room. Judging by the noises, he went through the hall and into another room, and returned carrying the jacket.

Ilmari took the jacket, very nearly snatched it from Salminen's hand.

'I'll just check on the rolls,' said Salminen. 'Can't let the cheese burn.'

While Salminen was in the kitchen, Ilmari checked his jacket pockets. The jacket seemed to be in good condition, though it had clearly been used. Salminen returned to the living room carrying a small tray with three glasses – the same ones with the ridge in the middle that they used in school cafeterias – and an almost-empty bottle of Whisky 88. He opened the bottle, divided the whisky equally, then handed the glasses to Ilmari and Antero.

'Nice to see you,' he said, and raised his glass.

Ilmari and Antero did not raise their glasses, with barely half a finger of the cheapest whisky around. Salminen knocked his own back; Ilmari and Antero wet their lips. Salminen smacked his lips. He seemed suddenly more alert.

'I used the jacket quite a bit,' he said. 'But it's none the worse for wear. Quite the opposite, actually. It's good for leather when it gets to move. It's a better jacket now. I've broken it in. Now it's ready to face the elements.'

Ilmari said nothing. He didn't agree with Salminen, but neither did he have any desire to get drawn into a conversation about it. Salminen was standing in the middle of the living room beneath a dark-brown plastic lampshade, and in this lighting Ilmari saw that his KISS T-shirt was so threadbare it was translucent.

'That was quite a gig,' said Salminen and again looked at Ilmari. 'I couldn't hear anything for three days.'

You certainly didn't hear the phone, thought Ilmari, and placed his glass on the coffee table.

'Thanks for the jacket,' he said. 'And the whisky. We've got to—'

'The rolls,' Salminen cut him off, spun around and disappeared into the kitchen.

Ilmari glanced at Antero, who shrugged his shoulders. Salminen returned carrying a baking tray and placed it on the coffee table. There was no denying that the smell of fresh ham and cheese rolls was tempting on a cold winter's day, even though they still had the food that Ilmari's aunt had packed for them.

And as strange as it felt, the smell made the room and the moment feel almost a little homely. Antero didn't stand on ceremony; he had already picked up a hot roll and folded it in two of his fingers. There appeared to be three, one for each of them. Ilmari decided to let his own roll cool first.

'I might as well tell you where I used the jacket,' Salminen began. 'When I was on stage. For me, it's first and foremost a performer's jacket.'

Ilmari didn't know whether to look at Salminen or the bread, and decided to look around him while Salminen continued theorising about the impact of clothing on a singer's performance. As an example, he named David Lee Roth from Van Halen, to whom – if Ilmari understood correctly, given he was only half listening – Salminen began comparing himself, especially the way he moved on stage.

The furniture, and its condition and sparsity, seemed to support Ilmari's theory that Salminen must have taken ownership of the property and its contents some time ago. There were obvious empty spots in the room where normally you would expect to see a table, a chair, a lamp or a painting. Ilmari didn't find it hard to imagine a scenario in which Salminen had sold all his furniture and other belongings one at a time in an attempt to fund his singing career, which, judging by everything around him, hadn't been quite the roaring success that Salminen had been hoping for. Ilmari noticed a pile of bills on the floor next to the armchair. They were easy to identify; Ilmari had received enough bills of his own. Not quite as many, maybe, and they certainly didn't lie around gathering dust like these. Ilmari caught the aroma of fresh bread again, looked down at the coffee table and saw his roll. He heard Antero swallowing the final mouthful of his own.

Ilmari was about to pick up the roll when he realised what he was looking at. He saw a delicious roll with quality fillings: the meat was fancy salami, the cheese looked like Emmenthal instead of Edam, and both of these were piled up very generously inside the roll. As if to make sure they were as attractive as possible. Which was in such stark contrast to everything else Ilmari could see around him. Why would an imaginary singer in an old, wafer-thin T-shirt who had sold all his belongings and lived amid piles of final demands offer two strangers who had come to pick up a long-lost jacket an expensive meal and insist that they ate it?

At the same time, Ilmari realised that while he was speaking, Salminen had slowly moved closer to the living-room window, and just then, at that very moment, he glanced out into the dark winter's evening, trying to do this as quickly and subtly as possible. Making sure Salminen didn't see that he was watching him, Ilmari managed to observe him glancing out a second time.

'Thanks for returning my jacket,' he said eventually, 'And it's been great hearing about your singing career. We've got some gear in the van. Stylish stuff. I wondered whether you might be interested.'

Salminen appeared to think about this. Ilmari could tell right away that he was interested but was holding back. Which, in its own way, confirmed Ilmari's conclusion that something wasn't right. Ilmari did not glance at Antero. He must know what Ilmari was talking about, but he said nothing. Ilmari thought he knew him well enough now to trust that they could work together.

'Stylish?' asked Salminen.

'Red and brown,' said Ilmari. 'Vintage stuff.'

'Hard rock?'

'And a heavy dose of Alice Cooper,' said Ilmari.

Ilmari could see in Salminen's eyes that temptation was overcoming caution. Ilmari stood up, glanced at Antero, who gave him a miniature nod of understanding, and making sure to keep the jacket with him and Salminen in front of him, they went into the hallway, put on their shoes and filed out into the snow. Now Ilmari knew that Antero understood his plan: they needed to take Salminen with them because he knew something, but they didn't have time to wait in the house to find out what.

Their breath steamed up in the cold; the snow looked yellow in the streetlight.

Only then did they see the car approaching.

We left in the nick of time after all, Ilmari thought to himself.

18

Every time someone spoke Swedish to Otto, it felt the same: like that person deliberately wanted to show that they were better than him – so much better that they had learnt some retarded language just to try and get one over on him. Otto didn't think it was very considerate, let alone friendly, which was what he strove for in all his interactions.

Even now, he had only stopped to buy some beer, to relieve himself against the wall in peace and to ask politely for directions, but he'd been forced to twist the passerby's arm behind his back – right up to the neck – just to get him to speak proper Finnish. And when the man had finally stammered a few confused instructions, his bad Finnish had made Otto so angry that he'd stuffed the man into a grit container.

But right now, he forgot all about that unpleasantness.

The van was right ahead of him.

He dropped his empty beer bottle out of the window and quickly assessed the situation. The streetlamps were on the left-hand side of the deserted road, so he pulled the car over to that side. The light would come from behind him and dazzle the twat driving the sofa. And it would look good too; he would arrive like Rocky or Rambo, surrounded in a halo of bright light, and what's more, it would all sound amazing, because he had wound the tape to exactly the right place for the occasion.

He braked, pressed play, turned the volume knob as far clockwise as it would go.

'Eye of the Tiger'.

Otto stopped the Saab on the left-hand side of the road, only fifteen or twenty metres away from the van. This was probably best, given the operation about to ensue. He took the shovel from the footwell on the passenger side and stepped out of the car as the music started playing. Everything looked and felt perfect. There were no witnesses – the whole place was empty of people and traffic.

But just as he was walking in front of the Saab, he was taken by surprise.

He hadn't expected...

Otto was confused and momentarily lost his sense of direction because...

Firstly, there were suddenly three men around the van. And one of them had just opened the back door, as if to unload the cargo, before Otto had given any kind of command to do so. Despite the loud music, to which he was singing along under his breath – *pah-pah-PAH* – he heard something else, something that didn't fit with his other observations. To cap it all off, he suddenly felt a strange trembling in the soles of his feet, and he only realised what it was when it was too late.

He managed to turn around, the shovel still in his hand.

Ilmari Nieminen recognised neither the dark-green Saab 96 nor the man who had got out of it. With his heavy winter boots, his long coat, his dour expression and small, red eyes, the man looked like an outlaw who had arrived on horseback, galloping across a wintery wilderness, eager for revenge. In his right hand he had a steel shovel, and he seemed keen to use it too. His engine was still running, and from the car came a loud, crackling version of a recent hit song whose name Ilmari couldn't remember.

Ilmari opened the last knot holding the back doors together and quickly glanced at Antero. Antero had read the situation correctly. He was standing behind Salminen, to make sure he didn't run off anywhere.

And while Ilmari was wondering how best to defend himself against a barbarian armed with a shovel, he saw – and heard – the sound of another car above the music.

This car was more familiar.

The egg-yolk-yellow Lada was driving towards them at speed, and if Ilmari saw correctly and wasn't simply imagining things, the car was being driven by the same long-haired individual in a red puffer jacket who had pointed a gun at him earlier. It was only right at the last moment that Ilmari realised the Lada had no intention of slowing down.

Time condensed, turned into fragments. It seemed to Ilmari as though he was following several events at once, each of them feeling dragged out, allowing him to watch them in great detail. In reality, everything happened almost simultaneously and in the space of a few seconds – ten heartbeats at most.

The engine roared, the hit song blared out and crackled.

The Lada slowed, but only a fraction, and perhaps only because it wanted to check its route. Which seemed to be directly towards the Outlaw. Now Ilmari could see right inside the Lada. He saw an older man whom he recognised as the one he had sent flying into the ditch. Then he saw a younger, dark-haired woman who once again seemed to be shouting something inside the Lada.

The Outlaw had turned, and for some reason appeared to have frozen on the spot.

Meanwhile, Salminen was on the move, trying to flee in the opposite direction, back towards the house. He only managed to take a step and a half before, with a single, laser-sharp kick, Antero managed to trip him up and topple him onto the snow. But instead of grabbing Salminen as he struggled in the snow,

Antero disappeared round to the other side of the van, out of sight. Ilmari lunged after Salminen.

The Lada struck the Outlaw. It was possible that Ilmari heard the slap, slam and smack of flesh against metal. He very vividly imagined the man and his shovel flying into the air, crashing down on the bonnet, the windscreen, whacking the roof of the car and continuing his rhythmless flight through the air like a crippled crow until he came down on the snowy road with a thwack. Of course, Ilmari might only have seen some of this and imagined the rest, as he now found himself wrestling in the snow with Salminen, who was surprisingly strong and had flown into a blind panic.

The Lada came to a stop. This Ilmari heard very clearly.

He managed to get Salminen in a headlock, clenched his arm tight and started dragging him back to the van.

To put it nicely, his previous plans had gone out the window.

Ilmari couldn't think more than half a second ahead. The van partially obscured his view of the Lada. Ilmari managed to get Salminen and himself back onto the road. He glanced to the left. The Outlaw was lying on the ground, the shovel next to him. Salminen was writhing and struggling, making Ilmari feel as though he was shepherding five drunken lunatics at once. Once he finally got back to the van, with Salminen's head still firmly locked under his armpit, he got a full view of what was happening.

And it was not what he was expecting.

Antero approached the Lada, stopped in front of it, and raised a shotgun onto his shoulder. The Lada's front bumper and lights exploded, the bonnet popped open, right away something started hissing and gurgling like a burst pipe. Antero took two steps to the left, reloaded the shotgun, and the Lada's front tyre met its Soviet maker.

The people in the Lada had begun to realise what was happening. The man and woman remained sitting inside and didn't even try to get out of the vehicle. Even Salminen had stopped thrashing around. Ilmari and Antero's eyes met; Antero gave a nod. Ilmari hauled Salminen round to the back of the van and bundled him inside. Salminen said something, Ilmari kicked him into the space at the back of the van, closed the doors, tied the thickest of the strings, then took three quick steps round to the driver's door.

He turned the Thames, reached across and opened the passenger door. He slid it into gear and picked up Antero, who was still aiming at the Lada, its passengers and its smoking engine. Ilmari looked right ahead and thought he would drive around the Outlaw lying on the ground. Except that he was no longer lying on the ground.

The Outlaw had risen to his feet, and he had the shovel in his hands once again. One half of his face was covered in blood, but the other half revealed that he was, if possible, even angrier than when he had arrived. And he was standing right in front of the Thames. Ilmari turned the steering wheel at the last minute. The shovel scraped the side of the van like the claw of a large animal. Ilmari accelerated, looked in the wing mirror. The Outlaw was standing facing them, but growing smaller in the mirror until he was barely visible. Only then did he turn away.

Ilmari and Antero arrived at a crossroads, heard Salminen frantically shouting something in the back but couldn't make out what. Eventually Ilmari chose the direction that felt the most improbable of all.

19

'The best steam money can buy,' promised the sign. The mock-up of a log sauna had been set up as a roadside advertisement at the far end of a recently ploughed lay-by, and there was just enough room for Ilmari to park the Thames neatly behind it, hidden from the main road. He got out of the van, walked round to the back doors, untied the knots and told Salminen to step out. At first, Salminen said he would prefer to stay in the vehicle, but upon seeing Antero and his shotgun, he reluctantly climbed out. On the one hand, Salminen looked like he was trying to maintain a sense of pride as he looked for the best place to stand behind the cold and stove-less sauna, but on the other as if it was finally dawning on him that there might be a difference between him and David Lee Roth after all.

'How long have you been in contact with them?' asked Ilmari. 'The Lada gang and the shovel man?'

Salminen shook his head. 'I don't know anything about them,' he said.

Ilmari glanced at Antero. Antero raised the barrel of the shotgun. Salminen took the hint.

'It was serendipity,' he said quickly. 'I mentioned your name to someone, said you were coming up here to fetch my gig jacket. And that was when, well, they made me an offer.'

Ilmari had no intention of getting into a conversation about the jacket.

'Who did you tell that I was coming here?' he asked.

'A mate in Helsinki,' said Salminen. 'When I mentioned you were coming to town, he said I could earn a bit of cash for that information, said there were people out there who would pay good money to know your whereabouts. I didn't mean for any of this to happen – people being run over and people shooting at cars. What you have to understand is, I'm about to buy a new microphone. Heavy ballads, brighter sound, Dio-style. I needed the money.'

Ilmari felt tired and annoyed. The remnants of all the excitement and exhilaration, he thought. He had used up all his strength and was now completely exhausted. But who wouldn't have been after a day like this?

'So when your mate in Helsinki told you someone would pay good money to know where I am and when,' he began, and he could hear the frustration and irritation in his voice, 'it didn't occur to you that you could be putting us all in danger?'

Salminen took a step back, as though Ilmari had suggested they dance together or something equally inappropriate under the circumstances.

'It all sounded professional and above board,' said Salminen, and now he sounded offended both for himself and the person who had given him the task. 'He was polite. Nobody mentioned bombs going off or anything like that, and he paid an advance too, just as he promised.'

Ilmari decided to bring the conversation back to what was most important right now.

'So, you called your mate in Helsinki,' he said. 'He put you in touch with someone else, who paid you for the information about my whereabouts, then passed it on, either to the people we have just encountered or to someone else. Correct?'

Salminen was clearly thinking hard.

'I suppose so,' he said eventually. 'That's what must have happened.'

Ilmari looked around, but all he could see was the stretch of illuminated road in the middle of the darkness: the road must start somewhere, and it undoubtedly ended somewhere too, but it did neither of those things here. He thought about what Salminen had said for a moment, then reached a decision.

'Okay,' he said. 'First, we're going to find a phone booth, then you are going to call the number that your mate in Helsinki gave you, and you're going to explain that the situation has changed, and we have decided to head south instead.'

'Really?' said Salminen, confused. 'South?'

Ilmari said nothing. It took an extra second before Salminen fully understood Ilmari's plan. Then he nodded, slow and deep, as though the penny had finally dropped.

'And once I've called him,' said Salminen, 'you'll let me go?'

'Once we get to Kilpisjärvi,' said Ilmari.

Salminen started vigorously shaking his head.

'No, no, no,' he said. 'I can't do anything like that. It's not ... possible. You saw what happened back at my place ... I can't lie to people like that.'

You've been lying to us all evening, thought Ilmari; just continue where you left off.

'Back into the van,' he told Salminen. 'We've got a long drive ahead.'

Salminen didn't move. Then he glanced at Antero. The barrel of the shotgun might have risen a fraction. Salminen gave a deep sigh, placed a foot on the back of the van and hauled himself inside.

Ilmari heard the sound of an approaching snowplough, which seemed to have arrived out of nowhere.

Ilmari turned to Antero. But before he could speak, Antero looked away and said:

'He's trying his luck again.'

Ilmari turned in time to see Salminen slip out of the van and disappear around the sauna. Ilmari ran after him right away, before he had consciously given his legs the command to go.

As soon as he reached the other side of the sauna, Ilmari realised quite how close the snowplough was. It would be right next to them in a matter of seconds. It was a so-called 'road bear', large and tall, and the driver was sitting almost two metres above the surface of the road. The front plough clanked and scraped the tarmac, casting tonnes of snow to one side, while an ice breaker stripped thick ice from the road. The ground seemed to shudder and sway with their combined force.

Salminen ran towards the plough, waving his arms, trying to flag it down.

At the same moment, Ilmari's attention was drawn to the driver's cab. The light was too bright. The driver was sitting in a curious position. Ilmari instantly realised what was going on: the driver had switched on the light inside the cab and was looking for something in the footwell. More to the point, the driver was looking neither at the road nor Salminen. He simply wasn't looking where he was going.

Yet there Salminen was – standing in front of an enormous snowplough, wildly waving both arms in the air.

Ilmari shouted to him, telling him to get off the road, said that the driver couldn't see him. He shouted at the top of his lungs, though he knew it was futile. The roar of the plough was like a small aircraft taking off or landing right next to them.

And then that aircraft landed.

Salminen understood the gravity of the situation a hundredth of a second too late. He managed to dodge the front plough but not the wider, middle plough, its steel teeth shrieking and shredding everything in sight. The teeth of a tool weighing several tonnes, and which was designed to remove layers of ice as hard as concrete from frozen tarmac, hungrily gripped Salminen and pulled him out of sight. Ilmari heard a simultaneous thud and a squelch, like throwing a large, ripe tomato at a wall.

Ilmari hurried to the roadside and got so close to the back of the plough that he felt the warmth of its engine. And that's when he saw Salminen anew.

He was smeared across the road in an even, dark-red streak that got longer as the plough continued on its way.

Ilmari wasn't an expert when it came to anatomy, but he could see there and then that Salminen's attempted escape had reached a dead end. His limbs and body parts separated from one another at sixty kilometres an hour, the plough's cab still shining like a lantern, the driver apparently still looking for whatever it was he was looking for. The chances of Salminen still being alive were almost nil, given his newly flattened and ever extending form.

Ilmari stood on the spot for a moment, then turned his attention to Salminen once again, who by now lay elongated over several hundred metres. He walked back to the sauna and the van parked behind it, and found Antero sitting between the back doors, half inside the vehicle, his shotgun beside him.

Ilmari stopped about two metres away from him and felt recent events weighing on him in a way that he couldn't recall having experienced before. He saw a quizzical expression in Antero's eyes.

'Change of plan?' said Antero.

Ilmari nodded but didn't say anything at first.

'Salminen...' he began, but didn't quite know how to continue, 'was uncooperative.'

Antero widened his eyes. They remained silent. Ilmari didn't know exactly where they had stopped, but the place was deserted regardless. Ilmari looked at Antero and felt his fatigue growing.

'You stole my aunt's shotgun,' he said eventually, surprised at the way the words burst out of his mouth. As if they had been on the tip of his tongue, getting ready to escape. Antero, meanwhile, didn't look at all surprised.

'I did what I promised I would do,' he said.

'Did you promise to shoot a Soviet car to smithereens?' asked Ilmari, now even more angrily. 'I don't remember anyone asking you to do that.'

Antero shook his head. 'I promised to take care of you.'

'You were carrying my aunt's shotgun without my knowledge,' said Ilmari. 'And you used it recklessly.'

'What would have happened, if I'd asked, "Is it okay with everyone if I take this shotgun and blow that Lada to kingdom come?"'

Ilmari knew the answer. He said nothing.

Antero continued. 'And what would have happened earlier on if, for instance, I'd asked you this morning if it was okay for me to borrow your aunt's shotgun because it just so happened to be the kind that can get you out of all kinds of tricky situations?'

'Is a shotgun the best way out of tricky situations?' asked Ilmari.

Antero thought about this. 'I don't see how we're in any position to negotiate right now.'

Of course, he was completely right. Yet Ilmari noticed how the unpleasant sensation inside him was still growing, drawing strength from somewhere far away.

'It's a question of trust,' he said.

Antero looked him in the eyes, then stood up. 'Is that what this is all about?' he asked. 'Okay, let's talk then. What do you want to know? There are no more weapons. We still have the food your aunt gave us and the body we were already carrying, but that's it. I might only have one leg, but I'm here and I know how to use a shotgun.'

Ilmari knew all of this. But it didn't ... And now Antero was nodding as though he had just heard some new information.

'Do you think I've got plans of my own for that sofa?'

'Well, do you?' Ilmari knew he had got to the root of the unpleasant feeling.

Something dark and shiny appeared in Antero's eyes. 'I just saved your life,' he said. 'And I've never told anyone else the truth about what happened on that train track.'

'But you don't have any money,' said Ilmari. 'Not even enough for a cup of coffee. And you know the sofa is valuable.'

'Again, how could I have been waiting for you at the petrol station in Pakila?'

'Did it have to be the petrol station in Pakila, though?' asked Ilmari. 'If you had an accomplice, and that accomplice had a car, you could have turned up at any petrol station.'

'In that case,' said Antero, and gestured to the shotgun, 'wouldn't it have been easier to simply steal the sofa? Why would I have jumped in the van with you and stayed with you, and done all this?'

Ilmari didn't have an answer. Antero took a step away from the shotgun, as if to demonstrate that Ilmari could take it from him if he wanted to.

'Like you said,' Antero continued, 'it's a question of trust. Maybe I should ask you the same.'

'Excuse me?'

'How do I know I can trust you?' asked Antero.

Despite his fatigue, Ilmari felt his agitation giving him strength and perhaps even perking him up a little, but not in a positive way.

'I'm doing what I said I would do,' he said. 'I'm driving a sofa to the north so I can buy a piano for my daughter in the south. You know that, and judging by everything that's happened, half of Finland seems to know it too.'

'I didn't mean that,' said Antero. 'I meant, what if I were the one in danger? Would you come to my rescue?'

Ilmari was taken aback, and though the hesitation lasted barely the blink of an eye, Antero noticed it. Antero turned, returned to the back doors, moved the shotgun and began tying the strings together. Ilmari was about to say something, but the agitation and the power it brought him had suddenly disappeared. Now all he felt was a profound fatigue – and the cold. The biting cold that chilled him to his bones.

'Salminen left his wallet,' said Antero. 'What do you want to do with it?'

Ilmari looked back the way they had come. They couldn't return to Salminen's house, and even if they did, who would they give the wallet to? Salminen had been living – and dreaming – alone. Besides, if there was any money in that wallet, it had been acquired by selling them out. Ilmari realised that his legs were beginning to tremble.

'How much money is in it?' he asked.

Antero opened the wallet and quickly counted the money.

'Okay,' said Ilmari. 'He was paid that money to betray us. Salminen got his microphone. I suggest we use what's left for a night at a motel. We need some rest. While it's still possible.'

Antero nodded, finished tying the strings together and climbed into the van. Ilmari made sure his legs would still carry him, then walked round to his own door, opened it and sat down in the driver's seat.

20

People were like warts: always in the wrong place at the wrong time and always unpleasant. Otto Puolanka bandaged his shin with the duct tape he had found in the boot and yanked his bone back into position. It hurt, of course, but not nearly as much as the thought that someone had run over him and that that someone had managed to get away, specifically because he hadn't been able to run after his assailants.

He pressed his bone with his right hand, and with his left tightened the tape. He noticed he was drooling with pain. He managed to get his shinbone into an acceptable position, placed a long-handled ice scraper against the bone as a splint and taped it on. Everything hurt, and blood was still dripping into his eyes from the gash on the top of his head.

Otto used up the entire roll of tape, some of it for the purpose at hand, some of it out of pure annoyance. Appropriately, his shin now looked like a ventilation duct running along a factory ceiling. He opened a bottle of beer; it tasted of blood and car paint. He lowered both front seats as far back as he could and lay down in the car almost diagonally. He succeeded in raising his leg, which was still throbbing painfully, onto the passenger seat and stared at a slice of the starry night sky through the window.

All of a sudden, it felt bad – lying in his cold Saab in the middle of nowhere. At first, he didn't know why; then he understood the reason. The sensation had plagued him for a while already. But now he realised what it was, and the full impact of this understanding blew his mind – and his heart. He had finally grasped it.

Everybody else had friends with them.

The hit-and-run wank-wads.

The furniture fuckwits.

Who were now far ahead of him, taunting him, flaunting their merry friendship to the world. Who were probably having interesting conversations in their cars, keeping each other company. Who helped each other, who could trust each other. And who, right now, were probably reminiscing about how much fun it was to run him over.

Meanwhile, Otto was travelling alone. Nobody did anything for him. Nobody was on his side.

What had happened a moment ago could have been a show of friendship too.

If they hadn't run over him, and if they hadn't run away and fled, Otto would simply have taken the sofa, and the van, and left, neatly and quickly – and he might not even have used his shovel at all. And in place of the van, he could have left the Saab – which, incidentally, he had stolen from a single parent. But no. That hadn't happened. For some people, nothing is ever good enough.

The world was an unjust place, and the people in it were even worse.

His eyes were stinging – and not just because they'd been doused in windscreen fluid from the Soviet banger that had run him over, he thought. They were stinging – no, *burning* – because he had always been treated so badly, and he was always so alone.

He looked up at the stars.

21

They only had enough money for one, shared room. They had a long, overly polite conversation about which of them could – or should – use the shower first, and Ilmari eventually convinced Antero to go in first. Ilmari lay down on the bed, heard the rush of the shower and closed his eyes. And instantly saw images that he wished he could forget. He opened his eyes and tried to find something in the room to look at. This was easy.

There were only a few items of furniture, and, with the exception of a solitary postcard, the yellowish-brown walls were bare. The lakeside scenery in the picture on the postcard was faded; the water in the lake would soon evaporate altogether. The room smelt of ingrained tobacco and the clicking radiator. The window gave onto woodland, the van was parked right in front of the window, and their room was at the back of the motel, so anyone looking from the main road would see neither them nor the van. Ilmari tried to come up with a plan for the following day and for the rest of the journey. But before he'd even started, it felt impossible. All he could do was try to reach Kilpisjärvi, one kilometre at a time, with the sofa intact; everything else was unpredictable. And this wasn't the only thing that was bothering him.

Once he got into the shower, he felt some relief: he didn't need to find something to look at in the room or something else to think about. The hot water pleasantly burned his skin, and as he warmed up, he perked up. He was still tired and needed some rest, but at least he wasn't shivering anymore. He returned to the room and found dinner laid out in front of him. Antero had placed the night table between the beds and set out Ilmari's aunt's packed lunch, napkins and all. Ilmari sat down at the table. Antero didn't look up and didn't say anything.

Antero's appetite seemed as healthy as ever. But Ilmari only nibbled half-heartedly at his liver-pâté sandwich. He took a small bite and tasted neither the liver pâté nor the ryebread, but something else altogether. He was suddenly painfully aware that here in this room were two men, sitting opposite each other, munching away, with much unsettled business between them. One of these unresolved matters Ilmari wanted to address there and then. He had been thinking of this while they were on the road, and now he was certain. What's more, he wanted to sound like he meant what he was about to say.

'You can trust me,' he said.

Antero looked up, gobbled down half a cold boiled egg.

'Good,' he said.

Antero continued munching, and Ilmari tried to make out something, anything, in Antero's expression that might show what he was thinking. But he saw nothing. Was the subject done and dusted now? Apparently so. Ilmari looked down at his sandwich. It still wasn't very appealing. Then he glanced outside and saw the van, which by now was more than just a van. He had already said one thing, so he could say another that had been weighing on his mind just as much.

'Can I ask you something?' he asked.

Antero interrupted his chewing, a piece of white bread and a slice of salami as thick as a fire blanket in his hand. Ilmari considered this pause as a sign that he could continue. He cleared his throat.

'There's no guarantee that we'll make it to Kilpisjärvi, with the sofa. So, if ... you make it there and I don't, then ... I'd really appreciate it if you'd fetch that piano from the instrument store.

It's black and shiny. Look for the lanky salesman – he's a composer. He'll have a copy of the agreement I signed. And deliver the piano to my daughter. I'll give you the address and phone number.'

Antero looked at him for a long while. The darkness seemed to have disappeared from his eyes and expression.

'Of course I'll fetch the piano,' he said finally. 'And of course I'll deliver it to your daughter.'

'Thank you,' said Ilmari. He waited a moment, then continued. 'What about you? Do you have any ... last wishes?'

Antero stopped, and Ilmari could see that the question had taken him by surprise, so much so that he blinked a few times, seemingly trying to find the right words before speaking.

'I'll have to think about it,' he said, before stuffing more bread into his mouth and lowering his eyes again.

Antero's reaction was unexpected. He was generally quite direct, sometimes to the point of bluntness; Ilmari couldn't remember seeing this kind of hesitation and uncertainty in him before. Ilmari was about to continue the conversation, but every question that popped into his head felt intrusive. Perhaps this was down to their fatigue: his mind kept winding back to where he had started a moment ago. To their conversation about trust. To trust in general.

'I must admit,' he began, 'I hadn't expected to find myself in a situation quite like this.'

Antero seemed to understand exactly what he meant.

'That's life,' he said, now without a hint of hesitation.

'Well, not quite,' said Ilmari. 'You start off delivering a sofa and you end up lying low in a motel in the middle of nowhere with a group of killers on your tail.'

'I mean that life is full of surprises,' said Antero. 'Plans change.'

Ilmari could hardly disagree.

22

Anneli Kukkorinne tried to move her toes inside her winter boots, but multiple pairs of woollen socks held them firmly in place. What was supposed to be keeping her warm was in fact making her even colder; it was working against its original purpose. Anneli wasn't sure whether this was an analogy for recent events and the thoughts they had aroused, but it was a distinct possibility. Her thoughts were rushing here, there and everywhere.

They had stopped at a remote farm to ask for directions. Anneli listened to the conversation between Erkki and a sleepy man whose woolly hat kept slipping over his eyes, but found herself thinking about communism instead, which was odd, given the time and place. What wasn't odd, however, was the question to which she kept returning as she considered various theories and their practical applications.

Trust. Ultimately, that's what communism was based upon, and that's why it worked. People needed trust everywhere: between the state and the people, of course, but between individual citizens too, between all peoples. Everybody should be able to trust everybody else, comrade to comrade. That was what made communism so beautiful.

And why did she always return to this same conclusion?

Because right now it felt like everything was falling apart.

Because right now there was no trust.

Anneli had had her suspicions about Erkki back in Helsinki, long before she had found the brochure for the auction house in the woods and noticed Erkki's strange behaviour in the toilets at the petrol station. But then their car had been vandalised. After which they had driven straight into an ambush. And to cap it all off, she had repeatedly been denied the opportunity to meet the Secretary or even talk to him. It felt as though the whole world knew something that she did not. She had tried to reason that the chaos she was currently experiencing must have something to do with her lack of sleep, the long, cold walk, the search for a telephone, stumbling upon this farm: all these things had worn her out, and all these things were facts. But try though she might, these facts did not change other facts.

Anneli listened as Erkki and the sleepy man negotiated a price: all this talk of money made them sound like unpleasant and distinctly suspicious businessmen blinded by capitalist dogma. Eventually they reached an agreement. And with that, they were on the move again. Anneli was pleased, not only for the cause but because of her toes. The yard had no lighting, and what little yellowish light there was came from the large log house nearby – into which they hadn't even been invited to warm up a little. What was more, the snow hadn't been properly ploughed, and they had to wade knee-deep in the drifts. So much for solidarity.

Erkki and the man in the yellow hat, who had introduced himself as Kale, had changed the subject and were now talking about ice hockey. Erkki said that Gretsky was destined to become the greatest player in history, but Kale thought him too delicate a boy for the men's game, and their conversation ended without reaching a conclusion. But soon afterwards, the men found something they could both agree on. And that was *Dallas*. Yet again, they didn't mean the city in the decadent United States but a television series that they both seemed to follow with worrying enthusiasm. Anneli wasn't aware of the details of the plot twists, but judging by the glimpses she had seen she knew more or less what it was about. Neither man thought much of

Bobby Ewing or Cliff Barnes, but they agreed that J.R. was of a different calibre altogether.

'Now there's a real man,' said Kale. 'Not some lily-livered lightweight.'

'No kidding,' Erkki agreed.

Anneli viewed their tastes as signs of ever-increasing degeneracy, and in Erkki's case it was particularly aggravating. To the extent that Anneli knew the character and understood his psychology, J.R. was a Texas chauvinist and an unscrupulous oil profiteer, for whom the only thing that mattered was money. Erkki's admiration for J.R. Ewing was symptomatic of a wider malaise, she thought, and it seemed to point in the same alarming direction as his curious words, his shiny brochures and his antics in public lavatories.

Eventually, they came to a halt. At first Anneli thought they must have stopped in the wrong place, that the men's excitement about the ins and outs of *Dallas* had made them take a wrong turning. But the men had stopped talking, and Anneli watched as Erkki sprang into action and took control of the situation.

And when the headlights lit up, Anneli felt new hope burgeoning inside her.

23

Within an hour, the snowfall that had started at six that morning had turned into a full-blown blizzard. They walked – first with the wind behind them, then with it blowing right into their faces – round to the back of the motel, and arrived at the van. Ilmari opened the door, climbed inside and turned on the engine. He opened the lock on the passenger door; Antero gripped the handle and slipped the shotgun, now wrapped in a blanket, on top of the dashboard. Ilmari waited for a moment and listened.

The engine started without any complaints and stayed running. Antero lifted their bags into the back. Ilmari brushed off the snow and scraped the frost from the windscreen, then wiped the ice from the wing mirrors, while Antero used the spade he had borrowed from the motel owner to clear the snow drift in front of the van. When Antero eventually went to return the spade, Ilmari sat down in the driver's seat and drove round to the motel's front door. Antero shook the snow from his shoulders and climbed inside.

'The owner says we're in for a storm,' said Antero. 'Says it's going to be the worst storm in a while. I told him we'll drive carefully.'

'About that,' said Ilmari. 'I think it would be best if we stuck to the main roads. They won't have time to plough the smaller ones, and the Thames wasn't designed for a rally through the snow.'

Antero agreed.

They drove west for a while, then turned north.

And they quickly realised that the main roads hadn't been ploughed either. The snowfall was thick, like a moving blanket

that they couldn't peer behind: it travelled with them, in front
of them at all times, tighter and tighter. Ilmari slowed more than
once, and before long they were travelling at the same speed as
they would in the town. No sooner were they able to focus on
any object ahead, than it disappeared into the white swirls. Ilmari
felt as though he were operating the car with his eyes closed,
fumbling his way forwards. And the Thames didn't seem to be
touching the surface of the road, as though a slippery rug were
rippling between the tyres and the tarmac. Ilmari noticed that
his eyes felt sore, and the world had turned into a giant,
shimmering fabric.

But neither of them suggested stopping.

First, they listened to Hanoi Rocks' *Bangkok Shocks, Saigon
Shakes* tape, then Dylan's *Desire* album. Dylan was perfect
listening for a snowstorm, thought Ilmari, though he was singing
about warmer times and climes. Every now and then, a gust of
wind shook the van, and Ilmari gripped the steering wheel a little
more tightly. Though the journey was difficult, they were making
good progress. Ilmari was content; so content that he now dared
think as far ahead as Rovaniemi.

There was another reason he was thinking about Rovaniemi.
It was to do with food. They had already eaten his aunt's
provisions – the last pieces of ryebread and the last slices of fresh
ham had been their breakfast – and after filling the tank again
they didn't have enough money left for food. But if Antero knew
some people in the town...

Ilmari wondered how best to broach the subject and decided
that asking directly was probably the best option. But Antero
didn't seem to hear him. Ilmari imagined this was because Dylan
was yearning for his Sara so loudly and so passionately. Ilmari
repeated the question, and this time Antero wiped the corner of
his mouth, as though he were eating.

'They're not, how should I put it...' he began, paused, then continued, '...the dinner-invitation type.'

Ilmari glanced at him. 'I don't mean to pry,' he said, 'but what's that supposed to mean?'

Again, Antero didn't answer right away. 'I suspect that we'll be better off trying to find food elsewhere. In fact, I don't just suspect it. It will be a far better and ... safer solution.'

'Fine,' said Ilmari, unable to hide the disappointment in his voice. 'If you're absolutely sure...'

'I'm sure,' said Antero, and he sounded like it too. 'I'm sure they don't have any food.'

For the next minute or two, Ilmari hoped that Antero would come up with a concrete suggestion of his own for how to solve their food problem, but he seemed even deeper in thought than before. And once Dylan finally got to the end of his song, Antero switched the tape to Led Zeppelin.

Ilmari had never visited Rovaniemi before, and he didn't know anybody in the town. He tried to think of some alternative solutions, but he found it increasingly difficult. Also, he had noticed that the Thames was getting through more petrol than he had initially calculated. He hadn't realised how heavy a load they would be carrying and couldn't have guessed how the bad conditions would affect their consumption. Which meant that, despite their lack of cash, they would have to refill the tank. One way or another.

And yet – despite the snowstorm, the increased fuel consumption and their other myriad challenges – everything felt a little more promising. Ilmari had slept well. They had survived a number of unexpected and tricky situations. And though undoubtedly there was still much more than just the road ahead lying in wait for them, nothing could be worse than what they had already experienced – surely.

Ilmari felt hopeful.

He turned to Antero and was about to say it out loud, when a massive boom came from the back of the van.

Ilmari and Antero flew up from their seats and hit their heads against the roof of the cab. The cassette player spat out the Zeppelin tape. Ilmari instinctively gripped the steering wheel with all his might. The rear end of the van rose into the air and came crashing down again, then rocked first to the left, then the right, then to the left again...

Ilmari had no time to think of anything, but instinct told him the only way to survive was to keep the van on the road and the bonnet facing forwards. He leant towards the windscreen, perhaps to see more clearly, perhaps to be more prepared – for what, he didn't know. Then, right away he realised that he knew only too well – and he slammed the accelerator to the floor, before he was even aware of doing so. From the corner of his eye, he saw Antero flash a look behind them. The Thames's engine howled and Ilmari clenched his fists around the steering wheel, and a second boom reverberated through the van. Someone had rammed them from behind, for a second time.

'A truck,' Antero shouted as the metal screeched and clanked, and the van jolted and shuddered. 'The bastards have got a damn truck now.'

Ilmari pushed his foot down on the accelerator, but it was already tight against the floor. The snow was getting heavier. Such was the nature of snowstorms. They were right in the thick of it. Every metre, every second meant less visibility. The Thames felt like it was speeding up, which meant they might have been going downhill. Not a very steep hill, but some kind of incline. Ilmari looked in the rearview mirror and couldn't see a thing. Then he gave a start.

Where were the truck's lights? Had the hill helped them lose their pursuers? How was that possible? Wouldn't the hill make the truck accelerate too?

The van's small engine howled. Suddenly, Ilmari felt a wave of cold air, and Antero again turned to look behind them.

'The doors,' Antero shouted. 'The doors have opened. And...'

Now Ilmari saw the truck. Right alongside them. Its tall, black flank and black tyres were perhaps only half a metre away. It was right up beside them. He heard the engine's roar, heard the driver changing gear. He could feel and hear the van's back doors swinging wide open, the tyres against the snow and ice. And he heard Antero.

'The sofa has come loose,' Antero shouted. 'The crash must have undone the ropes.'

The truck's flank was approaching, and Ilmari prepared himself for another impact. The Thames jolted again, rocked from side to side, but stayed on the road. Ilmari knew he was playing for time – a resource that was quickly running out. They needed to get rid of the truck, but he didn't know how. The snow was so thick that he couldn't see anything at all. Again, the truck appeared alongside them and knocked against them. Metal screeched against metal. The Thames remained on the road, though its right-hand side scraped along the snow-encrusted verge. Antero turned again, then turned back to Ilmari twice as fast.

'The sofa...' he said. 'It's gone.'

At first, the words didn't quite register; they felt wrong, out of place. Then Ilmari understood them, internalising the full force of what Antero had just said.

'When?' he asked once he was able to speak again.

'A while back,' said Antero. 'I saw a little signpost. We'll find the place.'

'A little signpost?'

'I'm pretty sure.'

'We can't stop now.'

'I know.'

Ilmari thought about things, he thought about them quickly, then told Antero what he wanted him to do and what he, Ilmari, was planning to do. Antero pulled out the shotgun, threw the blanket into the back of the van and placed the weapon between his legs. The truck was still right beside them, just as Ilmari had hoped. They must not allow the truck to fall behind them again. Whoever was in the truck must not find out that the sofa was no longer inside the Thames. But the truck mustn't be allowed to get in front of them either. As troublesome as it was, the current state of affairs was the best, under the circumstances.

The truck struck them again. The Thames screeched as its wing mirror was torn off.

Ilmari told Antero to get ready. Antero picked up the shotgun. Ilmari could hear and feel in his legs that the Thames's engine was starting to get tired. Though he still had the accelerator tight against the floor, the engine's strength was waning. Ilmari wound down his window as far as it would go. Cold air and snow engulfed the van, whipping them in the face. Their only hope was…

He saw a junction up ahead, perhaps a hundred metres away. In fact, he didn't see the junction or the slip road itself but a glimpse of the sign indicating it.

'Now,' he told Antero.

Antero leant over to the driver's side, almost lying in Ilmari's lap, aimed the barrel of the shotgun as far out of the window as possible. The weapon instantly had the desired effect. The truck fell back, swerved out of the way and disappeared into the blizzard, just as…

Ilmari turned the steering wheel a little and guided them onto the slip road. He did not take his foot off the accelerator. They were driving completely blind. Then the van's lights picked up another traffic sign, and Ilmari quickly braked. He tried to stop the tyres locking and managed to slow down while maintaining control of the vehicle. They entered the junction. Ilmari accelerated again, more carefully this time. The visibility was no better than it had been a moment ago. What was most important was keeping moving, preferably in the right direction.

The good news was that they were steadily putting distance between themselves and the truck, which was probably, and hopefully, continuing ahead in the heavy snowfall, without turning around. And though the truck would inevitably turn at some point, and though it would probably find the right junction and the right direction before long, Ilmari and Antero would no longer be there. Which meant that they had succeeded in shaking off their most imminent threat.

The bad news, however...

The storm forced them to stop. They had no idea where they were. They had tried to take a shortcut back to the spot where the sofa had disappeared, but after a while they had been forced to give up. Now they were sitting in the Thames, with fresh snow piling up on the roof and windows, listening to gusts of wind shaking the van. Ilmari switched on the engine at regular intervals. They had to keep warm, and right now the excess fuel consumption seemed like the least of their problems. Without the sofa, there would be no reason for them to drive all the way to Kilpisjärvi. Their journey would come to an abrupt end. And so would a few other things.

'Did the motel owner say anything about how long this storm is supposed to continue?' asked Ilmari, partly because he wanted to think about something else.

'He just said there was a storm coming in,' said Antero without looking up. 'Didn't say anything about the length.'

For a while, the two didn't speak.

'I must have left the doors open,' said Antero after a while. 'I mean, I didn't tighten the strings properly.'

Ilmari hadn't mentioned it once, not even when they had tied the strings again after stopping. And there was a reason.

'But remember who tied the sofa in place?' asked Ilmari. 'After we'd taken it out of the van and put it back in again?'

For a moment, Antero was silent. Then he nodded.

'Seems people can do anything,' he said. 'When they work together.'

They didn't quite laugh, but something in the air inside the van shifted. Ilmari took a deep breath, then slowly exhaled. He saw his breath steam up in front of him.

'Next time we're transporting bodies,' he said, 'we need to ask for a vehicle that won't let them escape.'

'And it would be nice,' said Antero, 'if they weren't the kind of bodies that everybody else wanted to get their hands on.'

'We'll put it in the contract,' said Ilmari. 'The bodies must be out of service in all respects and the vehicles need to be one hundred percent body-proof.'

'And I'd consider a clause about the weather too,' said Antero. 'In bad weather, bodies move more slowly and sometimes don't reach their destination.'

'Bodies travel at the sender's own risk,' said Ilmari. 'We're just shepherds: we guide the bodies in the right direction, but we don't give any guarantees.'

'Bodies,' said Antero, 'have a habit of going astray.'

'Bodies,' said Ilmari, 'were born free.'

Antero paused for a moment.

'I'm sorry,' he said eventually. 'For my part.'

'Me too,' Ilmari sighed. 'I'm sorry, for my part.'

Antero didn't answer. Ilmari started up the engine and let it idle until the cab was warm, then switched it off again. He leant his head between the edge of the door and the body of the van, found a suitable position and thought he would just close his eyes for a moment. He didn't think he would actually fall asleep, didn't think it was even possible, but that's what happened. He dreamt that he was asleep, next to his ex-wife, and even in the dream he wondered how it could possibly have happened. But because it had happened, he reached out to Tuulikki, wrapped an arm around her, pressed his face against her warm neck and almond-smelling hair and listened to the sound of her sleeping. Nice to have you home, she said, which Ilmari thought was strange, because he didn't know where he had been or how he had got home, or indeed that he had ever been away. He was about to ask her what she meant when he felt a tap on his shoulder.

'The snow,' said Antero. 'Looks like it's stopping.'

Ilmari opened his eyes. He expected to see the same relentless snowfall as before he'd fallen asleep. But the snowflakes were larger now, and there were markedly fewer of them. Somewhere there was even a flicker of blue sky. The landscape had assumed forms, details. There was a forest nearby. The spruces looked like spruces and not an impenetrable wall as dark as night; now they stood out from one another. Ilmari glanced at Antero and saw that he too had just woken up. He didn't understand how they could both have drifted off to sleep, and Antero looked just as surprised. Ilmari had no way of knowing whether Antero too had had strange, feverish dreams, but he felt sure that he had. He turned the key, and the engine stirred. He took the brush, got out of the van and waded round it, dusting the snow from the windows. He asked Antero to get into the driver's seat, while he walked round to the back of the van to push. After some initial difficulties, they managed to get the Thames out of the snowdrift, which had built up at the bus stop where they had parked, and back on the road.

The area was sparsely populated. They passed a few isolated houses with smoke rising from the chimneys like in childhood fairytales. They thanked fortune, providence and all possible divinities that the truck hadn't written off their small van. The absence of one mirror and one rear light and the partial loosening of the back bumper didn't even feel like losses. They still had a chance. Neither of them said it out loud, but Ilmari was sure that they were both thinking it.

Ilmari was again sitting in the driver's seat. They had switched over shortly after setting off. Ilmari had realised he wasn't able to wield the shotgun with the same level of accuracy as Antero, who, after thinking about it for half a second, had reached the same conclusion. After a while, they arrived at the spot where the sofa should have been.

But it was not.

This was the right place; of that, they were certain.

They saw the signpost, half buried in snow – *FRESH STRAWBERRIES, PICK 'EM YOURSELF* – though the directions for where to do this were obscured by the snow. If Ilmari and Antero had been looking for strawberries, they wouldn't have known which road to take. Apparently, the same applied to the lost sofa.

They got out of the van and headed off in different directions. They had only been walking for about a minute or so when Ilmari heard Antero give a shout. Ilmari turned, and hurried over to the spot where Antero was standing. He was pointing.

An area of snow, around fifteen square metres, had been churned up. Someone had trampled all over the snow, and something had been dragged across a collapsed snow verge and onto the road. The drag marks were long and even, extended right to the edge of the road and came to an end exactly where they were standing. Ilmari thought it wasn't an exaggeration to assume that someone had found the sofa and moved it first to the roadside, then taken ownership of it completely, either with the help of a rope or a car. Judging by the footsteps leaving the road and returning to it, this was the work of one person. But even though he knew all of this, he still knew next to nothing. There were already lots of tyre tracks on the road, meaning he couldn't use them to deduce anything, not even in which direction the vehicle had fled the scene.

Ilmari felt the air disappearing from his lungs, a cold fist gripping his stomach.

Don't let panic get the better of you, he thought, keep your thoughts on what you know and what you can work out. But still his thoughts were racing.

How can a person mislay the same sofa twice? In such a short space of time? And who steals a sofa that has obviously been lost in a blizzard and which is so clearly only temporarily missing? And more to the point: what kind of man steals another man's sofa? Another man's sofa with a third man hidden inside it?

Ilmari had to do something. He climbed up the verge, arduously trudging onwards as his feet sunk into the snow.

'The sofa isn't there anymore,' said Antero from behind him.

Ilmari didn't answer. He lifted his legs with difficulty and managed to reach the spot in the snow with the most footprints. Once there, he could clearly see the deep impression the sofa had left. He saw that it had been here quite recently too. There was only a thin layer of fresh snow in the imprint, like a veil of icing sugar, so whoever had taken the sofa must have got here at exactly the right moment, just as the storm was coming to an end.

'It was here,' said Ilmari.

'That's what I've been trying to say,' Antero replied. 'It might have been here, but it isn't any longer.'

Antero then asked Ilmari whether, like the sofa, they should consider getting out of here and trying to look somewhere the sofa might actually be, but Ilmari wasn't listening. His attention was drawn to something else, something the colour of snow and glistening like snow, but not snow. He waded a few metres towards it, crouched down, brushed the snow away and picked up...

A handle.

The plastic bag was torn and not even whole, but it wasn't

dirty or faded and clearly hadn't been left here over the winter; it was new, the plastic still fresh and shiny. It was entirely possible that this bag had been used to drag the sofa across the snow. That would have made sense. The bag's torn exterior confirmed this hypothesis: the sofa was heavy, and even if someone had managed to drag it, it would have ripped any plastic bag to shreds, even a strong one like this.

Ilmari laid the torn bag flat in his hands and noticed he was holding it the wrong way up. He turned the bag and read the text on the front.

'*Lahtinen*,' he read.

'Lahtinen?' asked Antero.

'Everything else has been ripped,' said Ilmari. 'There was obviously more text, but that part of the bag is missing.'

Antero climbed up the verge and started digging. They sieved the snow along the length of the drag marks where the sofa had been pulled back to the road. But they found nothing. Ilmari took the scrap of plastic bag from his jacket pocket, and they looked at it together.

It was their only lead.

25

Asking for directions was like standing in a shower of piss: just as useful and just as pleasant. In general. But now Otto Puolanka noticed that his interest had been piqued.

The man seemed to know a lot about the map he was showing Otto, and about the routes, which he had obviously taken many times himself. The man was younger than Otto, and his car – a gleaming white BMW 315 – was considerably sportier than Otto's Saab 96, which had the hint of a wet spruce tree. The man had spread the map out across the bonnet of his car and was moving his finger along one of its many lines.

'But if you take this route,' he said, 'you can drive as fast as you want. I've never seen a single police car along the whole length of that road. If you keep to a steady hundred kilometres an hour, you'll gain half an hour compared to the main road.'

The man continued outlining the route, but Otto was already sold. The man didn't seem at all interested in why Otto's face looked like a half-demolished house. The bumps and bruises stood out all the more clearly now that he had washed his face in the snow.

'So, if I want to catch up with my friend,' said Otto, 'I should drive straight to Kilpisjärvi?'

At first, the man said this was right, but then he began to hesitate. Otto noticed this and didn't like what he saw.

'But what?' he asked.

'Well,' the man stammered, again placing a finger on the map. 'You said your friend likes a good practical joke...?'

'He's trying to trick me and have a laugh at my expense,' said

Otto. 'I'm supposed to be following him, and he wants to make it as hard as possible. Between you and me, he's a bit of a prankster.'

'Right,' said the young man. 'In that case, I think he'll almost certainly drive via Rovaniemi, though it's a bit out of the way. But only a bit. And that will give him more opportunities to try and trick you, if he really wants to put you off his trail.'

'He doesn't want to lose me altogether,' said Otto. 'I mean, no one wants to get rid of their friends for good.'

'In that case,' said the man, now tapping different spots on the map, 'I would take the quicker route I showed you all the way to Rovaniemi and wait there. You'll be there in no time, and I guarantee you'll give your friend a shock. And if he doesn't drive that way after all, you can still get to Kilpisjärvi by taking this detour here and keeping your speed nice and steady.'

Otto stood upright. They were standing by the petrol tanks at a service station in a small industrial area, and Otto felt something that he couldn't remember feeling before. Perhaps he'd never felt it. This man had helped him, without asking for anything or demanding anything in return. Otto looked at the man, his cropped fair hair jutting in all possible directions. His grey eyes suggested a certain slowness, but a far greater loyalty too.

'What do you want?' asked Otto.

'How do you mean? It's no problem to give you directions,' said the man, confused. 'I had a map, and—'

'In life, I mean,' said Otto. 'In general. What do you want?'

Otto decided it was important not to lose his temper with the one and only person that he wanted to help in return. He waited. The man looked around him and eventually seemed to understand the question.

'I want to keep this car,' he said with a shake of the hand. 'I don't want to have to give it back to the dealers. But I'm behind with the repayments.'

Otto thought for a moment.

'Where is the car dealer?'

The man turned a fraction and again waved his hand. The car dealership was diagonally in front of them on the other side of the road, only a few hundred metres away. The premises appeared dark and closed. Otto looked at it for a moment, then returned his attention to the young man.

'You can keep your car,' he said.

The man didn't seem to understand what he had heard, so Otto repeated it, thanked him once more for his help and said goodbye, then sat down in his own car and turned on the engine. The man did the same at the other side of the petrol tank: he started his BMW, gave Otto a confused wave, and disappeared from the forecourt. Otto watched his departure, and once the man and his car were out of sight, Otto switched off his engine and got out of the car. He took the canister he had picked up earlier and filled it with petrol, took a screwdriver from the boot of the car and slid it into his pocket, then sat back down in the car, started the engine, and this time drove off the forecourt.

Fifteen minutes later, having used his hefty screwdriver to break into the car dealership via a side door, he emptied the contents of the canister all over the premises. Then he returned to the side door, lit a Camel cigarette, took a deep breath, enjoying the combined aroma of petrol, cars and tobacco. He stood in the dark, quiet store, lost in thought, smoking his cigarette until there was only half of it left. Then he flicked the burning end as far as he could and backed out of the door.

He was already sitting in his car when the premises exploded.

He saw the glow of flames in his rearview mirror and felt a warmth inside him. But this wasn't the warmth of the fire.

It was the warmth of friendship, of returning a favour.

26

They tried everything. First they leafed through the telephone directory and called all possible Lahtinens, which in practice meant all companies and stores registered under the name Lahtinen within the local area that might conceivably have their own plastic bags. Two of them did, but one had yellow bags and the other blue bags. Neither of them had ever even considered making white Lahtinen bags. By the time he had called all these numbers, Ilmari's stash of one-mark coins was greatly depleted. He and Antero then drove to a nearby Spar, showed the bag to people in the car park and asked whether it looked familiar. They quickly noted two things: nobody recognised the bag, but more than that, most people they asked seemed to find their behaviour more than a little odd. They left the car park and moved to the village pub. Nobody recognised the bag in the pub either, but their hopes came alive when one of the four customers said it reminded him of something. Ilmari and Antero ordered pints of beer – Ilmari paid with a handful of one-mark coins – and waited. Eventually, the man said that maybe he was mistaken after all, maybe he was thinking of Koskinen's store instead. Ilmari and Antero took their pints and moved to a table by the window.

Once installed at their table, they tried to think of an alternative way to solve their problem. What if they just got another sofa? But then they would still be short of a body. And even if they could get their hands on a random body, it wouldn't be the body the recipient was expecting. What if they drove all the way to Kilpisjärvi and negotiated a new contract? Even in the slightly surreal atmosphere of a shabby old pub, it didn't feel like a very realistic option. What if they took out an ad in the local paper asking if anyone had seen a missing sofa? They quickly concluded that they might as well take out an ad saying they were going directly to jail without passing Go, because that's what would happen if the sofa were to fall into the wrong hands.

Their conversation dried up.

For the most part, the view out to the road running through the village was as still as a postcard panorama. Few people seemed to have any business in the village, or anywhere else. Ilmari allowed his eyes to pan along the even verges of snow piled up along the roadside but his enjoyment of the view was constantly interrupted by restless thoughts. He tried to avoid the most unpleasant ones, but it was impossible. He felt the same exhaustion as before, but now it was laced with a sense of fear and contrition.

They both tried to start up the conversation again, a little lighter this time, as though they were just two friends sitting in a pub having a pint. It felt distinctly unnatural. It was hard to talk in any great depth about football or rock music when you could feel the cold barrel of a gun against your forehead. A lame discussion about Arsenal and a dispirited Bowie analysis fell flat, and eventually they gave up. Ilmari told himself that, despite all his dark thoughts, he mustn't lose hope. They just needed a miracle.

There was only one reason that Ilmari noticed the dark-coloured van.

Antero had started leafing through the evening tabloid, not so much reading it as flapping the pages back and forth, which meant Ilmari had to lift his pint glass higher than usual to be able to enjoy his beer. The raised pint glass first reflected the van's front lights, then, as it turned, its side. Something about the shape of the vehicle made Ilmari turn in his chair, and he saw the car from behind, under the light of the streetlamps, just before it disappeared again.

A moment was all it took.

He saw the van from an angle, and only for a hundredth of a second, but he was sure of what he had spotted. The word *Lahtinen* on the van's side – in exactly the same font as on the plastic bag they had found.

'Let's go,' he said.

They left their pints on the table, ran to their van and sped off towards the highway. Ilmari could feel his heart racing in frantic, furious beats, and he had to grip the steering wheel to keep the van on the road and himself in the seat. They were driving well over the speed limit and heading almost directly east, which meant yet another detour.

They caught up with the other van on a dark stretch of road. Ilmari kept a suitable distance, but close enough that, as the road veered to the left, they were able to see the text on the van's side again. He confirmed his earlier observation: *Lahtinen's Buy and Sell*. Ilmari felt a wave of relief and jubilation. He knew this might be premature but concluded that at least they were actually *doing* something, which was better than merely sitting in a pub with a pint. At the same time, he realised why he hadn't found the company in the phone directory: this company had a different area code.

They followed the large van for over an hour, all the way to the company's buy-and-sell warehouse. The dark-coloured van turned onto the forecourt in front of a sheet-metal building. Ilmari switched off the Thames's lights and drove past. Shortly afterwards, he headed back and drove closer to the building, stopping a good distance away. He switched off the engine, and they waited. They were about sixty metres from the warehouse, between them nothing but a stretch of trees, both large and small, all stripped bare by the winter. Among them were a couple of spruces that blocked their sight line and hid their position. This was good.

Ilmari couldn't tell whether Antero was holding his breath or not. Ilmari certainly was.

They could see two men. One of them was standing by the van's back doors, which were open, while the other was opening the sliding door at the front of the building. The latter man disappeared inside the building for a moment, then a large, bright floodlight lit up the forecourt. The men first carried a large dining set into the warehouse: six chairs and a heavy-looking table. After this, they each picked up a large mirror, reflecting light here and there through the evening dim like shooting stars. Then it had to be time for the sofa. As Ilmari and Antero knew only too well, this was a two-man job. Ilmari noticed he was sweating, and his heart felt like a drum that someone else was beating.

The men managed to lift a piece of furniture out of the van, and Ilmari and Antero recognised it instantly. It was their sofa. They quickly glanced at each other, then looked at the men, who had placed the sofa on the ground and looked like they were talking. An hour ago, Ilmari had prayed for a miracle, and now he asked for another one. He hoped that the sofa would remain in one piece and the body would remain inside it. The men gripped the sofa again, lifted it and disappeared inside the warehouse. Ilmari could hear the thump of his heartbeat in his ears.

They waited. It felt like a long wait. Then it felt too long. Only once the men reappeared on the forecourt did Ilmari dare to take a breath. And when they gripped the other pieces of furniture and began carrying them indoors, Ilmari started pulling the sweaty shirt from his skin and tried to relax his upper body. He felt as though he had been carrying something too.

The men finally managed to empty the van. The floodlight was switched off, and when the men got back inside their vehicle, Ilmari started the Thames's engine. He reversed and turned the van without switching on the lights, then drove away from the warehouse for around five minutes. Then he steered the van into a ploughed bus stop at the side of the road and switched off the engine. The men's van did not pass them, so it must have headed in the other direction.

Ilmari and Antero sat in the cold van. They knew what lay ahead. They knew what they had to do.

27

To Ilmari, the words 'breaking and entering' instantly sounded bad. He didn't want to break into anything, and Antero didn't seem especially keen either, but they calmly accepted the reality of the situation. Ilmari had to admit that once again they were low on options. They simply didn't have the money to buy the sofa back. And even if they did, turning up at the warehouse and negotiating with the men who had stolen it felt far too risky. Besides, they didn't have time to do it. Breaking into the warehouse was the only way of getting the sofa back into their van within their tight schedule. Nevertheless, Ilmari only made the final decision once he had come up with a plan to compensate the buy-and-sell outlet for any damage it might incur. He wrote down the name of the outlet and that of the village they had just seen on the signpost. He would work out the exact address later on and send the required sum of money in the post as soon as possible, and this he would do anonymously. Antero gave an affirmative nod, then reminded him of the situation in which they now found themselves: the temperature in the van was quickly dropping, and they were still one sofa short of a suite.

It quickly became apparent that neither of them had any previous experience of breaking and entering, and it seemed not even Antero's background with the Foreign Legion could provide a quick fix. They decided to take it one step at a time.

They left the van at a suitable distance and walked the rest of the way. They wanted to make sure they could get into the building before pulling up in front of the door and potentially drawing attention to their nocturnal wheeling and dealing.

The winter's night was cold, the moonlight bright, and the temperature a bracing minus twenty. Their breath steamed in the air, their toes tingled inside their shoes.

The sheet-metal warehouse was unheated, primarily intended for storage. First, they inspected the heavy-duty padlock on the sliding doors and quickly decided it wasn't worth wasting time trying to crack it open.

They walked around the building. The snow had been properly ploughed on three sides; only the rusty back wall facing the woodland had been left untouched, the snow still lying a metre thick. And because the three, five-metre walls around which it was easy to walk didn't offer any chance of getting inside, once again they found themselves wading through knee-high snow.

Along the back wall they found a join between two sections of sheet metal that, for whatever reason, looked a little loose. It seemed this would be their only chance. They got to work moving snow out of the way, and realised that the deeper into the snow they dug, the looser the join appeared. They shovelled the snow with their hands, heaving it away from the wall. The working conditions were challenging: the snow was a metre deep, and they had no tools to speak of, never mind a real spade. Ilmari's gloves were soaked with snow and sweat, letting the cold come right through them and numbing his fingers. Antero didn't say anything, but Ilmari assumed he was in much the same predicament.

They managed to shovel away the snow right down to the foot of the wall and saw that, at floor level, the sheet metal was completely separated from the rest of the wall. They combined their strength and managed to bend the sheet metal back, pulling it loose from the rest of the construction until there was a gap between the corrugated iron to the side and the concrete flooring underneath just big enough for a man to get through. There was only one problem: it took two men to hold the wall open. Which meant neither of them could slip inside the building. And they couldn't exactly go back to the village and ask for an extra pair of hands. They relaxed their grip on the sheet metal and caught their breath.

They stood in the snowdrift, moonlight illuminated the rusty wall, everything was perfectly silent. The cold permeated their bodies; there wasn't a single spot where the frozen air didn't hurt. They hadn't eaten for a long time. Losing hope can be a physical sensation too, thought Ilmari, and it felt like this: chilled to the bone and faced with endless setbacks.

Antero sat, or rather plonked himself, down in the snow. Ilmari understood him. But Antero didn't remain in a sitting position. He worked fast, took off his trousers, put them on again, and stood up once more, only this time with some difficulty: he was holding his prosthetic leg.

Again, they gripped the loose sheet metal, its sharp edges. They worked together, bent it backwards, this time pulling it even further away from the rest of the structure. Ilmari felt his muscles trembling, then the lactic acid started to stiffen them, as though some greater power had simply frozen him on the spot. Nonetheless, he tried to tighten his grip, and once he thought he had as good a grip on the sheet metal as he was likely to have, he shouted, 'Now.'

Antero let go of the sheet metal, grabbed his prosthesis, which he had left ready and waiting, lunged forwards and jammed it between the wall and the ground. And almost immediately, Ilmari's hands let go, not of his own volition, but because the lactic acid had rendered them numb and completely powerless. He staggered backwards and landed on his back in the snow; he tried to get up but couldn't. He managed to roll onto his side

and noticed that the sheet-metal wall didn't look the same
anymore and that Antero was currently crawling through the
narrow gap and into the building. Ilmari looked up at the sky
and thought he could see stars.

The stars were real: they were twinkling brightly as Ilmari
trudged to the corner of the building, reached the ploughed
section and forced himself to jog to the other side. He heard the
metal of the sliding doors screech, saw Antero's face in the
moonlight. A moment later, they were both inside the
warehouse. Ilmari pulled the door shut behind him. They
switched on the only light fixture in the space, hundreds of items
of furniture came into view, and they instantly identified the one
piece they had come to collect.

'You get the car,' said Antero. 'I'll put my leg back on.'

Ilmari ran again. He started the engine, drove the van right
up in front of the main door. He hadn't seen or, more to the
point, heard a single other vehicle while they had been working
at the back of the building. If everything went to plan, they
would be able to drive out of the yard without anybody seeing
them.

Ilmari went back inside the warehouse, and heard Antero at
the other end of the space, behind the furniture.

'My leg's stuck,' he said.

Ilmari walked over to him and saw what had happened. The
sheet-metal wall was holding Antero's prosthesis hostage. They
had to find something to push the metal with, and push it hard.
Because the wall was completely stuck. The wall and the
prosthesis had formed a tension of their own, one that was much
stronger than the sum of its parts. Ilmari ran off into the
warehouse looking for something, though he didn't quite know
what. Anything, anything at all.

He returned to the doors through which he had entered the building and saw a platform trolley. He wheeled it around the warehouse, loading it up with the heaviest items he could find. Then he pushed the trolley closer to the problematic wall and cleared himself a twenty-metre runway in front of it, so he could accelerate enough. All this took time and energy, and Ilmari was more than aware that both were in very short supply. Eventually, he had cleared the way, and the platform trolley was ready for action.

But, as Antero pointed out, the task wasn't quite that simple.

If this trick worked, the wall would come off in its entirety. This, in turn, would probably cause a sound not unlike a small explosion, which might draw some attention on this quiet and perfectly idyllic winter's night.

'I'm out of ideas,' sighed Ilmari.

Antero looked first at his prosthesis, then the wall, then the loaded platform trolley.

'As soon as you're done, we need to leg it.' he said.

'Mate,' said Ilmari, 'pull the other one.'

But this was no time for wooden-leg jokes.

Ilmari gripped the handle, made sure he was holding it tightly, crouched down, and pushed with all his remaining strength. The trolley started moving. Every step required extra effort, and he gave it everything he had. The trolley began to gather speed, and eventually Ilmari felt that, instead of him pushing it, it had started to pull him, faster and faster. And just before the trolley with its heavy load struck the wall, Ilmari hoped they were wrong about the noise of the impact.

They were not.

The platform trolley slammed into the wall, and the sheet metal separated from the rest of the structure as though it had been blasted off. The sound was anything but a small explosion.

It was a dull, booming, screeching sound that echoed through the winter's night like cannon fire.

Ilmari dashed to the other side of the warehouse to slide open the door at the loading bay. Meanwhile, Antero worked quickly. He reattached his wooden leg and was on the move again. They approached the sofa, quickly decided who would do what and in what order, then positioned themselves at opposite ends. They crouched down and made sure they both had a firm grip. Then they lifted the sofa.

It was too easy. Too light.

Quickly and instinctively, Ilmari wondered whether something earth-shattering could have happened while he was wrestling with the metal wall, whether the exertion had increased his strength exponentially, fundamentally changing the physical dynamics between him and the rest of the world. Perhaps Antero was experiencing the same. But then the truth of the matter washed over them like a river bursting its banks – or a similarly devastating natural phenomenon. They stopped in their tracks and stood for a few seconds in perfect silence, the sofa still in their hands. They both knew what had happened.

The sofa was just a sofa.

The body was missing.

Ilmari's heart, which only a moment ago had been beating furiously in his chest, had now stopped altogether, and he could feel his rumbling stomach filling with cold, foreboding oil. Ilmari was facing forwards, his back to the sofa, and couldn't see Antero. He made a decision.

'Let's take the sofa back to the van,' he said.

They carried the sofa to the van, loaded it into the back, pushing it as far back as it would go, attached it tightly and closed the doors, carefully tying the strings together. They had barely sat down in the cab when they heard the blare of sirens. They rolled down the windows, trying to hear which direction the police were coming from. Then Ilmari switched on the engine, and they set off in the opposite direction, driving slowly and quietly through the moonlit night.

28

Anneli Kukkorinne flinched as she realised she was gripping the handle of her pistol, hard. It had happened by itself; she had been lost in thought, and her hand had slipped into her pocket without her noticing. Anneli forced herself to loosen her grip – which was surprisingly difficult – then she took her hand out of her pocket, slipped it into her mitten and turned her attention once again to Erkki, who was right now ordering them some hot *lihapiirakka* minced-meat turnovers.

The truck was parked some distance away. The deserted square with its dark, low-rise buildings felt more like outer space than the centre of a small town. The impression came partly from the bright moonlight and the network of stars glowing across the other half of the sky, which both served to highlight the sense of emptiness spreading across the world. But Anneli thought the reason for what had happened was somewhere else.

They had failed, yet again. They had managed to get themselves another vehicle, and they had located the van. They had driven alongside it, so close that Anneli could almost have touched the sofa. Then she had shouted 'Shotgun', and Erkki had veered away from the van, and then ... nothing. The snowstorm had swallowed up everything in the landscape, and eventually it had swallowed them too. They had stopped and waited for the storm to pass, and once the snow had abated, they had tried to drive back the way they had come, but it quickly started to feel like they were going in the wrong direction after all.

Because, thought Anneli, you can't travel back in time. In more ways than one.

When this journey finally comes to an end, she would try even harder to move on. She would get rid of Erkki, one way or another. Yes, she would work with the Secretary directly and answer only to him. There was no watered-down version of the revolution.

Again, she noticed she had taken the mitten off her right hand and was gripping the handle of her pistol, now even more tightly than before. She was still holding the pistol in her hand when she heard Erkki's voice.

'All the toppings?'

She looked at Erkki, saw his stony face in the cloud of hot air steaming out of the hatch at the fast-food kiosk, and nodded. Erkki turned back to the hatch and, despite his expressionlessness, he looked like he was enjoying himself, visiting a fast-food kiosk late at night and everything that entailed. He ordered himself something to drink – half a litre of milk – and asked what Anneli wanted. She looked at the list and asked for a carton of raspberry juice. Erkki paid for everything, handed Anneli her meat pie. She hesitated, left the pistol in her pocket and took the food. The pie felt like a warm, moist pillow in her hand, soft and heavy.

'That'll cheer you up,' said Erkki as they walked to a small table outside the kiosk.

Anneli looked at the table, the thirty centimetres of snow on top of it, then at the steaming, greasy pie in her hand. Erkki started munching on his own pie. Because it was hot and the sausages inside it even hotter, he ate with his mouth open and washed everything down with cold milk. The combined sound of these two actions was like that of a large ship turning in the harbour. Anneli didn't know how the pile of food in her left hand would ever end up in her stomach.

'How do you know we can afford this?' she asked.

She waited for him to swallow his mouthful of pie and milk.

'It's on me,' he said. 'My treat.'

Anneli shook her head, was about to say that she meant more generally, in terms of time, when Erkki nodded to show that he had understood.

'I already told you,' he said, preparing to take another bite of his pie. 'We're ahead of them.'

'But how can you be so sure?'

'We've always taken the most direct route, sometimes gone back and forth along the same stretch of road, and we've always been going faster than the speed limit,' he said, licking mustard from his thumb. 'So we know they must have taken a detour. At this point, that automatically means that we're ahead of them. And we know the hand-over will be in Kilpisjärvi. When you look at these facts in the cold light of day, it's logical. And besides … the Secretary agrees.'

Upon hearing these words, Anneli flinched, but she managed not to show it. She definitely hadn't misheard him; she knew exactly what Erkki had just said. She quickly thought through recent events and tried to put them in order. They hadn't stopped anywhere where there might have been a telephone box. She was sure of this. Erkki could not have talked to the Secretary. It was quite simply impossible.

'Really?' she replied.

Erkki nodded. 'We just need to keep cool heads.' In the yellow light of the streetlamps, Anneli saw the mass of rice and meat in Erkki's mouth. 'And focus on the sofa.'

Anneli waited a moment before speaking.

'Good,' she said. 'Excellent. I trust the Secretary. And you, of course.'

Erkki continued eating.

'Do you and the Secretary,' she began, 'have a plan for when we arrive in Kilpisjärvi?'

'Depends on the terrain,' said Erkki. 'We'll know when we get there.'

'The Secretary won't be with us,' she said. 'And it's a sparsely populated area. There might not be a phone box for miles.'

Erkki stopped chewing but didn't take his eyes off his pie.

'Good point,' he said. 'We'll have to bear that in mind. I'll have to ... ring before we get there.'

'I'll remind you,' said Anneli.

'Thank you,' said Erkki.

Anneli looked around. They were the only people outside. There was one person sitting inside the fast-food kiosk, and the doors at the bus station were about to close behind someone else. Anneli looked at Erkki once again and thought she might finally be on to something. But what? What was this all about? But just when she was about to ask another question – though she wasn't quite sure how to formulate it – Erkki burped and said:

'You all right?'

Anneli was taken aback but reminded herself that, though she was suspicious of Erkki, she didn't want Erkki to be suspicious of *her*. At all.

'Of course,' she said. 'Long live the revolution...'

'I meant the pie,' he said. 'You're not eating. It's a good pie.'

Anneli looked first at her supper, then at Erkki.

'I'm just waiting for it to cool down,' she said and forced herself to bite into the warm dough.

Just as she had taken that bite and started moving it from one side of her mouth to the other, Erkki shifted position and put down what was left of his own pie as though placing it on the snow-covered table for inspection. Or sacrifice.

'There's something I have to tell you,' he said. He looked and sounded somehow different now. 'Something I've never told anybody before.'

Anneli's mouth was full of mustard and pickled gherkins. Her right hand let go of the pie, slipped into her pocket and touched the handle of her gun. Erkki looked around. Or perhaps he wasn't so much looking around as observing the immediate vicinity. That's it, she thought. He's checking their surroundings. Anneli suddenly felt her heartbeat higher in her body than usual, in her ears, and she wished her mouth wasn't full of food. What would she do if Erkki told her? Told her *what* exactly? That he wasn't really a communist? That he had joined the enemy? All of a sudden, anything was possible.

'I've been living with my sister for two years,' he began, and lowered his eyes to his meat pie, or rather, as Anneli could now see, what was left of it. 'Ever since Airi threw me out.'

Anneli expected him to continue, but he didn't. She didn't know what to say. She was still gripping the gun, and now her mouth was full of cooling carbohydrate.

'The good food made me think of it,' he continued. 'I just thought I'd tell you.'

'I'm sorry,' she mumbled, as her tongue couldn't move properly for all the stodge. 'Sorry to hear that.'

Erkki nodded, and they looked each other in the eyes. As always, Erkki was impossible to read. This didn't stop her from trying, though. She wondered whether this too was one of Erkki's diversion tactics. Because, as soon as he had made his confession, *his* right hand had slipped into *his* right-hand pocket – where he always kept his trusty knife. While Anneli was gripping her pistol, he was gripping his knife. And both stood holding their meat pies. The moment seemed to last an eternity.

Eventually, Erkki looked away. He licked his pie's wrapping paper, and perhaps he too was staring at the same deserted market square as she had a moment ago. He turned but didn't quite present his back to her, keeping her in sight out of the corner of his eye.

His right hand was still in his pocket.

29

They drove slowly, keeping their eyes on the right-hand side of the road. Then they arrived at the spot (naturally, they could make only a very rough estimate of this) where the truck had rammed them from behind, tearing open the back doors in the process. Ilmari slowed even further, and by now the Thames was travelling at walking pace. Antero said he thought it was unlikely that the body would have leapt out of the sofa and flown out of the van at the first impact like a very stiff jack-in-the-box. Ilmari asked whether Antero had any better suggestions about where they should start looking for the body. He did not. They were both impatient, and they realised they were getting desperate. And they had another problem too.

The bright moonlight of a moment ago, making everything look like the negative of a photograph, was now only a fleeting luxury: clouds seemed to have appeared out of nowhere, just to taunt them. Of course, this wasn't actually the case. Ilmari knew that the clouds didn't have a personal animus towards him or Antero, or even the missing body of the crime boss. They just floated across the skies, probably unaware of where they were or, indeed, what they were, before changing shape and continuing on their way...

Ilmari realised that his thoughts had started to wander. He was still wet from rolling about in all that snow, and he felt like he had run a marathon, then spent a few hours lifting weights. He forced himself to concentrate on the dusky, snowy embankment. Which seemed endless. The fact was that they had spent the last several kilometres looking for a silent man, 175cm tall, hiding horizontally under layers of snow.

Eventually, they accepted there was no way there were going to find what they were looking for by simply milling around like winter tourists. They would have to roll up their sleeves and get their hands dirty. Which meant they would have to start digging again.

They put their hopes in the places they had already been. That seemed the most probable solution. It felt logical to assume that the sofa had flown out of the van and bounced to the place where the trail had led them earlier that day, and that at some point during that flight, it had released the man hidden inside it. Ilmari wondered whether finding the body would have affected the men who had moved the sofa into the warehouse. He thought it would. They would have behaved differently, and he was a hundred-percent certain they would have called the police, because they had no special relation to the deceased that might lead them to try and cover it up. Which meant the body was here somewhere. It had to be.

They divided up the search area and got to work.

There wasn't much going for this place, but one positive thing was the lack of traffic. They didn't want to draw attention to themselves, especially now that the police were looking for whoever had just burgled the buy-and-sell warehouse on the other side of town. Whenever a car approached them, which happened extremely rarely, they tried to look like two men who had pulled over to answer the call of nature.

They continued to wade back and forth through the snow, and Ilmari didn't know whether it was possible to get any wetter than he already was. Snow pushed its way all around his body, through his clothes, between the layers. And then it melted. He had to keep moving, otherwise the cold started to feel too terminal. Every now and then the moon disappeared behind the clouds, but their eyes quickly became accustomed to the shadow world around them, and they continued their search.

And so they searched until they had gone over as large an area as they could imagine the body could have travelled. It was unrealistic to assume that the body had flown hundreds of metres through the air. The man hadn't been fired from a cannon; he had fallen from a moving sofa. But once again, they were exhausted.

They returned to the van, Ilmari started the engine, and they both held their hands near the heater. They took turns drinking currant juice from the canister Ilmari's aunt had given them.

'You know one of the reasons I joined the Legion?' asked Antero.

'What's that?'

'I've never liked snow.'

'Understandable,' said Ilmari.

They sat in silence. Antero held the canister in his lap.

'Is it true what your aunt said about you and your wife?' he asked.

Ilmari turned slightly. He couldn't remember his aunt mentioning Tuulikki, and certainly not in Antero's presence.

'What do you mean?' he asked. 'What did she say?'

Antero didn't answer at first.

'That you'd separated or something like that,' said Antero after a pause. 'Maybe I misunderstood. Of course, it's none of my—'

'I made a mistake,' said Ilmari.

He didn't know where the words had come from. But he knew that they were true. Antero said nothing. Ilmari tasted the currants and the sugar in his mouth, and something else too.

'Well, I don't know whether it was a mistake, as such,' he continued. 'It was just something that I ... did. I kept Tuulikki at a distance. And the more I should have trusted her, the greater the distance became. Eventually, I moved out. You could call that a mistake. With a capital M. I've never said this out loud before.

So, in answer to your question ... yes, it is true. It's my fault. All of it.'

'Maybe you can still do something about it.'

'I doubt it,' said Ilmari. 'And now there's some Lauri in the picture.'

'Lauri?'

'Yes.'

'And how long has this Lauri been ... in the picture?'

'I don't know,' said Ilmari, though he knew only too well. 'A year and a half, maybe. They meet every now and then.'

Antero said nothing. Ilmari turned, looked at him. The clouds had retreated from in front of the moon, and it looked as though Antero was smiling.

'Never thought I'd meet anyone who understands human relationships even worse than me,' said Antero. 'But it looks like I've met my match. And I'm the one who lay down on the train tracks, remember. If dating for a year and a half hasn't led to anything, it won't ever lead to anything. With all due respect to this Lauri.'

Ilmari looked at Antero a moment longer, then turned away.

'We need to find that body,' he said.

'We need to get back home,' said Antero.

Ilmari realised that the words had slipped out of Antero's mouth, burst out just like his own words a moment ago, and that they were just as true as his.

'I guess I assumed you didn't have a home,' he said. 'Judging by what you've told me.'

'Generally speaking,' said Antero, without turning to look at Ilmari, 'I don't.'

They sat in silence. They had drunk almost three litres of juice, virtually emptying the canister. Ilmari thought this might give them just enough energy to continue for a moment. He didn't

want to think about what would happen once his last drop of
energy was gone. Another problem was fuel. The needle on the
indicator was edging its way dangerously towards *E*. Even now,
they were using up petrol that they could ill afford to waste.
Soon, they wouldn't have enough fuel to get them to the nearest
petrol station. Ilmari tried to soak up the last gasps of the heater,
then switched off the engine. He glanced at Antero and knew
without saying anything that he too understood the situation.
Ilmari pulled on his wet mittens.

'We're going to have to widen our search,' he said. 'We divide
the terrain into sectors, each of us moves towards the road, and
whoever finds the body first gives a shout.'

'When it snows, it blizzards, right?' said Antero and opened
the door.

The moon was giving way to the sun, morning was breaking over
the horizon, the night's clouds had disappeared. It was going to
be a clear day. An hour later the sky was gleaming a bright blue.
Ilmari could see Antero as a small dot at the other end of the
road. He could only make him out because Antero was moving,
while the rest of the landscape remained still. He remembered
what Antero had said about snow, and he was ready to say the
same.

He was pondering their conversation more broadly. He was
thinking about Tuulikki again and remembered that he had
recently dreamt about her too. At first he tried to push these
thoughts to one side, telling himself that he was tired and in a
desperate situation, and that was why he was raking over past
deeds, but he had to admit to himself that it hadn't just been
about the circumstances. He really had made a mistake. And
now, in wet clothes in the middle of a forest in northern Finland,
he had the feeling that he was paying for it. He raised his legs,

reached the embankment, dropped down to the roadside, started walking back to the van and gave Antero a wave. Antero saw him, and Ilmari watched as the small dot began moving from the woods and out to the edge of the road.

Then, all of a sudden, Ilmari sensed his legs trembling, and he felt dizzy. The temporary energy from the currant juice was gone. He stopped and imagined he was leaning against the van. At least, he had intended to lean against the van's battered flank, but the van wasn't there. He hadn't reached it yet, though he'd thought he had. He raised his eyes and looked up at the sky. Morning had broken more quickly than he had thought possible. Thin filaments of light danced here and there across the crusted snow, making it sparkle like millions of tiny diamonds all around him. The rays of light began to exude warmth, Ilmari was sure of it. He was shivering with cold, and the cold hurt, but over there it would be warmer. Besides, there was no point going to the van. They couldn't switch on the engine. The van wouldn't offer any heat.

Ilmari stopped.

Light filtered between the trees, making the snow gleam and glisten in strips.

Ilmari clambered back over the embankment, reached the snow once again, sank into it and continued on his way, towards the warmth. He felt as though he had warmed up long before he reached the particular beam of sunlight he had been aiming for all the way from the road. The one where the morning light appeared to have burst into flame. He took off his mittens, held out his stiff, frozen fingers and imagined himself holding them above a fire, carefully so as not to burn himself. He heard Antero asking something. It didn't feel important. What could be more important than this warm place he had found?

He held his fingers closer to the fire, waited for the heat to seep into him, and was surprised when it did not. He looked more closely and saw the flames flickering on the surface of the snow. It looked like fire; it had to be fire. He stuck his hand into the fire and held his fingers there until they started to hurt. Then he realised something was wrong. He moved his hands, turned them in the bright light. Eventually, he had to raise them and look at them. They were covered in snow. He looked at the fire he had found. It wasn't there.

All that remained was the winter, the crusted snow glistering in the frozen morning.

Ilmari stood on the spot and couldn't help the tears that began to well in his eyes. First one, right in the corner of his eye, then another, running down his cheek. Then they started coming more quickly. He shivered with cold. Antero asked whether he was all right. Ilmari turned to look at the sun. It was rising in the sky. At the same moment, he knew he was about to fall, and decided not to try and stop it. He was on his back in the snow, his eyes bleary with tears, and the sun would not warm him.

He had lost Tuulikki because he deserved to lose her, he thought. He was dying because he deserved to die. If not of cold or hunger or thirst, then because he wasn't able to keep hold of sofas and cadavers. Which was extraordinary, as humans could tame lions and conquer mountains, but who had ever heard of a man who could tame and conquer neither a sofa nor a corpse? Nobody, of course.

Ilmari saw the sky, which looked both blue and wet, but maybe it was just his eyes. He thought of the piano, its shiny black flanks, and of Helena. The only shiny black flanks she would see would be those of his coffin.

The sun was shining brightly, and he had to turn his head. Now he could no longer see the fire or the flames, but there was something in the snow, something still, something shining differently in what he had thought was a sea of fire. It gradually assumed a form, its own unique surface and reflection. In a flash, Ilmari knew what he was looking at. He knew what was protruding from the snow.

A nose.

30

Rovaniemi was beautiful, and it was a beautiful day. Otto had a friend. This friend was not with him, however, but he was with him in spirit. Which, right now, felt like almost the same thing. Because now Otto knew what friendship was. Of course, it meant exploding cars, yes, and shops engulfed in flames, but more than anything it meant having a shared direction of travel, mutual goals, a selfless ability to help each other, and an understanding of what people needed.

Otto couldn't remember ever feeling excited about anything in his life, but the thought that somewhere out there his next friend was waiting for him gave him an inkling of what excitement might feel like. He wasn't entirely sure, but something about his thinking had changed, and he found himself looking at the sky above the low-rise business premises and seeing, not the approaching darkness, but different shades of blue, from the faint light along the horizon to the deepness of the sky.

His excitement was laced with another emotion too – a new, tingling sensation.

He wanted to tell the people who had just run over him about his discovery, the attractive young woman and the old codger, and the couple of clowns who were still hiding the sofa from him. He wanted to tell them that now he knew what companionship felt like, and that, in his own way, he had joined their number. Of course, he would have to add that they couldn't become his friends, for the reasons just outlined, but that he wanted them to know he was no longer lonely and that they shouldn't laugh at his earlier loneliness. And only then, after making them understand this, would he give them what they had coming.

Otto drank from a bottle of Koskenkorva, took a long, deep gulp, screwed the top back in place and wiped his mouth. He lit a cigarette, smoked it down to the filter, then stuffed the butt into the already overflowing ashtray. He was ready to see the doctor.

He had chosen a private clinic. He didn't like the public health service, not because he hadn't received good care there but because they would have records of him that he didn't like and that always led to questions that he didn't want to answer.

The single-storey building was long, its roof low. Of its five business premises, the doctor's reception was in the middle. To its left was a hardware store, to its right a knitting shop. At one end of the building was a bar, and at the other end a sports shop. The doctor's glass-and-metal door didn't open when he tried the handle, so Otto pushed the white plastic buzzer on the wall.

The doctor himself opened the door. Otto could tell he was the doctor by his coat and the badge pinned to his lapel. He was a curly-haired, slightly breathless man who looked first surprised, then a little worried, and finally both. He asked whether Otto had booked an appointment. Otto didn't answer and stepped instead into the small waiting room, pulling the door shut behind him. He looked around and listened. He could neither see nor hear anybody or anything. He pointed at his leg and said it was getting sorer by the minute, which made it hard for him to carry out his job. He added that he needed his leg back in working order rather quickly as he had a business meeting for which he simply could not be late.

'I'm a dentist,' said the man.

Otto told the doctor he could check his teeth too, if there was time, but that right now he had to focus on where the pain was coming from, namely his leg. Otto walked the man into the main surgery, complete with a dentist's chair. He locked the door, sat the doctor down on his stool and lay down in the dentist's chair. The doctor looked like it was only now dawning on him what was happening, and Otto saw him quickly look at the door.

'Friend,' asked Otto. 'Or fuzz?'

'Pardon me?'

'You've heard the saying: the police are supposed to be our best friends?'

The doctor looked like he really had to think about it. Otto thought this curious; you'd imagine someone with a medical qualification would know things like this. Eventually, the doctor nodded and said he had indeed heard it.

'I changed it a bit,' said Otto.

'Really?'

'So you can choose: friend or fuzz.'

The doctor looked at Otto, and Otto hoped he would make the right decision. Otto had started, and now he wanted to gather as many new friends as he could. He didn't want to end up in a situation whereby he had to foreclose on potential friendships because of the potential friends' bad decisions. After a moment, the doctor looked at him.

'Perhaps I might start by removing that duct tape and taking the ice scraper off your shin,' he said.

Otto felt a hint of the same sensation he had experienced in the company of his friend who was worrying about the finance on his car. Promising, he thought.

The doctor took a pair of scissors, cut the duct tape and, with Otto's permission, his trousers too. Then he stared at Otto's violet-black shin, stood up from his chair and fetched tools and equipment from three different cabinets. He then numbed Otto's leg and, when Otto asked for more pain relief, ad-

ministered a second shot of anaesthetic. This was the main reason
Otto had come here. He needed painkillers. He had work to do,
he had to be able to move freely.

Then the doctor got to work.

He cleaned the long wound – an open gash, to be precise –
but said he wouldn't be able to do anything about the missing
piece of shinbone. Otto told him not to worry about that, adding
that there were plenty of other pieces of bone floating loose
around his body. The doctor was about to ask something else but
didn't. He stitched up the gash, bandaged Otto's shin and began
washing his hands. Otto got up from the chair. His leg felt odd,
and walking required a lot of effort, but the pain no longer
prevented him from moving around. He was ready.

Otto stopped at the door.

'Friend,' he said.

The doctor nodded right away, without a moment's hesitation.
'Friend,' he replied. And he sounded happy, as though he was one
hundred percent sure of the matter.

Otto looked at the doctor, then turned and left the room. As
he pulled the door shut behind him, he noticed the reception
desk in the waiting room and the bright-yellow telephone sitting
on it. He walked to the front door, turned the lock, pushed the
door open, then stopped.

He heard the doctor's upbeat response over and over.

The door closed in front of him.

Otto did not hang about.

He silently returned to the desk and crouched down behind
it. He didn't have to wait long. The door to the surgery room
opened. Otto heard two hesitant steps. Once the doctor had
concluded that the reception was empty, he dashed to the desk,
muttered something to himself, picked up the phone and dialled
a number. Only three digits.

Otto knew what that meant.

He stood up from behind the desk, pressed a finger on the switch hook, cutting off the call. The doctor dropped the handset and began to back away. Otto followed him into the surgery and couldn't help feeling a pang of disappointment. At first, the feeling was small, then it started to grow and spread, until it felt like a black wave drowning out the pleasant feeling he had had before. Soon, it was gone and all Otto could feel was disappointment, rejection and, eventually, anger.

'Friend,' said the doctor, but now he didn't sound quite as sure or upbeat about it.

Otto said nothing.

All he could think was how much he had always liked the sound of the dentist's drill.

31

They ordered schnitzels. They couldn't afford them, but they ordered them all the same, and the wait for their food felt like a lifetime. They were sitting at a table by the window, for one reason and one reason only: they would be able to see if anyone other than a regular customer looking for petrol drove onto the forecourt. They were particularly on the lookout for any trucks and Saab 96s. Neither of them had any interest in the wintry landscape.

Again, Ilmari noted Antero's dishevelled appearance: he looked like he had been dragged through both a concrete mixer and a washing machine but hadn't been straightened out after the wash. Ilmari knew he probably looked the same. He had tried to tidy himself up in the petrol-station toilet, but it was hard to do anything about his tattered clothes, his profound fatigue and his face, chapped from the cold. You can't simply wash that away, not even with the paper towels in the toilet that were as rough as sandpaper. From time to time – in fact with great regularity – at least one of them looked out of the window to check that the van was still there.

Their schnitzels arrived. They ate heartily, bent over their plates like cavemen, their hands and jaws moving fast. Right now, they *were* cavemen. They were like ancient wanderers carrying their dead through perilous terrain to a special resting place. At least, that was what Ilmari thought as he fetched his complimentary cup of coffee from a pot that looked like it had been standing next to the till since the dawn of Finnish independence. The waiter visited their table and cleared away the empty plates.

In the cafeteria's loudspeakers, Rudolph guided his sleigh through a winter wonderland.

Ilmari felt the afterglow of food and warmth. He felt languid, invigorated and suddenly alert. He looked at Antero, who was stirring what must have been a fourth sugar cube into his coffee. Ilmari couldn't help smiling.

'Looks like we're a pretty good team after all,' he said.

Antero didn't answer.

'You think?' he said eventually.

Ilmari nodded. 'Absolutely,' he said. 'Think of everything we've been through.'

Antero looked like he was giving this consideration, then nodded too. 'You're right,' he admitted. 'Nice to hear you think the same.'

Ilmari waited a moment then continued. 'And I want to say, I'm sorry for what I said earlier about ... That I suspected you of stealing, all those years ago ... for so long.'

Antero stopped stirring his coffee, placed his spoon on the plate next to his cup. He was quiet for a moment, and perfectly still. Then he looked Ilmari in the eyes.

'I did take that money,' he said.

'What?'

'The money for the camp,' said Antero. 'All those years ago. You were right. It was me.'

'Is this a joke?'

'I don't think so.'

Ilmari kept his fingers on the handle of his coffee cup but didn't raise it to his lips.

'Why...?' he asked and tried to continue the question, but it was pointless. The question was only one word long because that was the whole question.

'I was trying to help,' said Antero.

'Help?'

'Yes. My mother was ill. The kind of leukaemia that doesn't respond to any treatment. Then she heard about this clinic in Denmark where a patient had survived the exact same cancer as she had. But it was expensive, and we didn't have any money. My father was only interested in himself and his cars. Which has come in quite handy these last couple of days. But my aim was to get together enough money so my mother could go to Denmark.'

'And did she?'

'No,' said Antero. 'My father used the money to buy a wrecked old Mercury. I can fix those too, if you've got one.'

Ilmari shook his head. 'I don't have a Mercury,' he said. 'And I'm sorry. I just ... didn't know.'

'The coach knew,' said Antero. 'I told him everything. He didn't really blame me. I think he was angrier at my father. I think that's why he arranged those interviews, so the whole thing would look like it had run into a dead-end and would forever remain a mystery. The thing is, Uimonen forgot to invite me to his interviews, and eventually the story got out that I had refused to take part. And there were consequences for that. But he did visit my mother in hospital, though. Then she died, and I never saw him again.'

'I vaguely remember,' said Ilmari, 'somebody saying you'd moved in with your father a bit further away.'

'If by "a bit further", you mean a thousand kilometres away,' Antero nodded, 'then, yes. To Rovaniemi. My mother and father were originally from Rovaniemi, but they left before I was born. It was an alien place to me. I lived there for a few years, then joined the Legion at eighteen.'

'And your father is still in Rovaniemi?'

Antero glanced out of the window, started stirring his coffee again.

'Yes, he's still there,' he nodded.

Ilmari looked out of the window too, again checking the position of the van. The body was still firmly inside the sofa, the sofa firmly in the van, the van's doors were tied tightly shut, and the van was where they had left it.

'Still, I owe you an apology,' said Ilmari. 'For then and now.'

'Apology accepted,' said Antero quickly. 'Nature calls.'

He stood up, and Ilmari sipped his coffee, which suddenly tasted neither bad nor bitter. It had cooled a little, so he got up from the table and walked to the counter, refilled his cup, and was about to return to the table when he happened to glance towards the toilets. He saw Antero on the phone. He imagined he was probably calling Rovaniemi, telling someone about his arrival, and thought that maybe he should call someone too. 'Should' being the operative word. He didn't know how he could call Tuulikki these days except by calling Helena, and that was out of the question. When he called Helena, he called Helena. She had never been a go-between for him and Tuulikki and never would be. Besides, what exactly would he say to Tuulikki?

Listen, I'm sorry about what happened in the past, but transporting a body around the country, being in constant mortal danger, meeting a certain singer from Vaasa who ran in front of a snowplough and seeing him smeared along the highway have really opened my eyes, and now I can see I've been running away from you and myself, and my old friend, who used to be in the Foreign Legion, almost killed himself, but he's a dab hand with a shotgun, and through his example he's made me understand the value of reconciliation...

Maybe not.

Ilmari sat at the table and was drinking his coffee when Antero returned.

'According to the weather forecast, it's a beautiful day in Rovaniemi,' he said. 'But it's going to start snowing again later.'

Antero's announcement meant that the momentary warmth and relief that Ilmari had felt were now gone for good. And it wasn't just fear and premonitions about the weather that Ilmari had pushed from his mind; there were other things he had managed to forget about too.

'The gang that are after us,' said Ilmari. 'They're probably ahead of us by now. They'll be waiting somewhere.'

'I think that's highly likely,' Antero nodded. 'It took us a while to find the sofa and the body. And I guess they'll be paid upon delivery too, and not before.'

'That means the truck with those two lunatics,' said Ilmari. 'Then there's the Sergio Leone wannabe. When I saw him standing up after being run over...'

'Hard to imagine he would have stayed there,' said Antero. 'But if there's a silver lining, they all know where we're going and are probably already in Kilpisjärvi or at least on the way there, and they'll be waiting for us. And we won't meet them until we get there.'

Ilmari sighed. Antero was probably right. And though postponing the inevitable didn't solve any of their problems, at least it gave them some time to think.

'One more thing,' said Ilmari after a pause. 'We just ate our petrol money. We've got half a tank of fuel, and that's enough to get to Rovaniemi, but then we have to come up with a way of getting some more.'

Antero looked at the van outside.

'Once we've taken care of this stop in Rovaniemi,' he said eventually, 'it'll be easier to think about other things. I'm sure we'll be able to find some more petrol. Something will come up.'

32

The ninety-minute drive to Rovaniemi felt uncannily easy: the roads had been properly ploughed, the snowfall had paused, nobody was trying to run them off the road. However, as soon as they set off, a rattling sound appeared on the left side of the Thames – the flank that had sustained the battering – but it didn't seem to affect the vehicle or the driving. After listening to the metal rattling for ten minutes, Ilmari suggested that Antero choose some music for the ride. Antero examined the collection of cassettes at his feet and slid a tape into the machine. Ilmari was surprised at the choice.

'I didn't take you for a Dire Straits man,' he said.

'I'm not a Dire Straits man,' said Antero without turning his head. 'But this new album feels appropriate under the circumstances.'

The way in which Antero said this told Ilmari that there was no room for further questions. Besides, there was no need for them. Antero's story at the petrol station had cleared up many things. *Love over Gold* began with the fourteen-minute 'Telegraph Road', and Ilmari had to admit that, in some way, it really did suit the mood.

They crossed the River Kemi and arrived in Rovaniemi. Antero gave the directions. They drove through the city centre, checking their surroundings all the while. Though they were nearly one hundred percent sure that they would only encounter new problems once they headed north to Kilpisjärvi, they still had to be on their guard. They saw people here and there, some in winter attire and clearly heading to the cross-country skiing tracks, but they didn't see their pursuers or anything else that might arouse suspicion or alarm, and they successfully managed to leave the city centre behind them. There were fewer houses now, and they were generously spaced. Ilmari was preparing to slow down and turn into a driveway. Antero continued giving instructions. Take a left here, now straight on, a right over there, straight ahead. As he did so, Antero's tone of voice changed, assuming a new, sharper edge.

Eventually, Antero said that they could slow and look for a parking spot by the right-hand side of the road. And soon, once they had passed the trees, Ilmari saw a short, narrow parking area. He carefully steered the van over a small, snowy verge and stopped but didn't switch off the engine.

'Now where?' he asked.

Antero did not turn to look at him but kept staring directly ahead.

'Nowhere,' he said, and now his voice was both sharp and cold. 'We're here.'

Ilmari quickly looked around him. Apart from the Thames, the parking area was deserted this winter's evening. But that wasn't the only thing that felt odd. The houses with their illuminated windows were further off on the other side of the road, and there would have been plenty of room to park there too, either in a driveway or at the side of the road. But Ilmari had been concentrating on the houses and hadn't even looked at this side of the road – the side on which they were parked. And for good reason too, he now thought, as he looked straight ahead.

'This is a cemetery,' he said.

Ilmari turned his head and saw Antero. It was impossible to read his profile.

'Like I said,' Antero replied, 'we're here.'

'What about your father?'

'He's here.'

'You mean,' Ilmari gave it one more try, 'he works here?'

'He's here,' said Antero. 'Dead and buried.'

Ilmari looked at Antero for a moment more, stared, in fact, then turned and looked ahead again. At first, he wasn't sure what he felt, as all the conversations he'd had with Antero played through his mind on fast-forward and he heard both Antero's words and his own. But then he knew what he felt. And it wasn't far from rage.

'So, he's dead,' Ilmari heard himself saying.

'Has been for a long time,' said Antero.

'How long?'

'It's been ten years,' said Antero, 'and much longer since my mother died, of course.'

Ilmari took a deep breath. 'And we absolutely had to come here?' he asked. 'I don't want to sound callous, and I certainly don't want to offend you at a moment like this, but if your father has been dead for ten years—'

'I've never visited him here,' said Antero. 'Like I told you, I left Rovaniemi when I was eighteen. And I didn't keep in touch with him. I haven't once visited his grave.'

Only now did Ilmari realise he was still gripping the steering wheel. He released his chilled fingers.

'That's...' he began, and though he tried his hardest to make sure the annoyance still smouldering within him didn't make its way into his voice, he could still hear it. 'That's understandable. But I don't think you've been entirely honest.'

'About what?'

'You said...' said Ilmari. 'You left out a rather important detail. Again, I don't want to be insensitive, but the fact of the matter is that we have a gang of killers on our tail and, frankly, your father could have waited for this visit a while longer. He's dead, after all, and he has been for some time, like you said. Why couldn't you have waited until we drove back this way?'

Antero turned to look at Ilmari. 'Because by then I might be dead too.'

Ilmari was about to say something but stopped himself. He had to admit that Antero was right. The truth wasn't particularly pleasant, but it was still the truth. They were transporting a dead man; now they were visiting a dead man; and they might soon be dead men themselves. Ilmari had to use all his will power to dismiss the thought. He switched off the engine.

Antero said nothing more, pulled on his mittens, which, like Ilmari's, now stank of oil because they had dried them on top of an oil heater at the petrol station. Antero got out of the van, took a few determined steps towards the cemetery gates. Ilmari watched him go, then took his own oil-smelling mittens from his jacket pocket, pulled on his oil-smelling woolly hat, locked the van's door and followed Antero into the graveyard.

The lights in the cemetery only illuminated the main pathways. They walked to the end of one such path, then turned down an almost pitch-dark pathway between two lamps. The thick spruces, dozens of pines and the occasional birch formed irregular but all the more impenetrable walls around them. With each step, Ilmari wasn't entirely sure where he was about to place his foot. He asked Antero how he knew where his father was buried. Antero explained that he had called the cemetery caretaker and enquired about it, then committed the coordinates to memory. He added that he was rather good at this; the Legion had taught him how to do it, the hard way. Ilmari decided not to ask for the details.

The pathway grew narrower. Ilmari positioned himself behind Antero and followed him. The snow had crept back into their shoes. They were suddenly surrounded by tall trees, and clearly in a part of the cemetery that was barely used. Antero stopped; Ilmari did the same. The faint yellow light from the main pathway barely lit this area. Ilmari felt as though he was standing simultaneously in a thick fog and a forest in the grip of winter.

Antero moved his hand and eyes slowly and rhythmically, as though he was counting the gravestones protruding from the snow. They started walking again, then Antero headed right into a drift of crusted snow, and after a few steps, he crouched down and began dusting the snow from one of the gravestones. Eventually, he stopped, gave the gravestone one last wipe and straightened his back. Ilmari's eyes had become accustomed to the dim, and he saw the name on the stone.

NIILO KUIKKA.

He couldn't make out the dates or the years, but right now they didn't feel important. Niilo Kuikka was firmly underground and had apparently been there for a considerable time. Neither of them said anything. Then Ilmari saw the air steam in front of Antero's mouth, and looking more closely he was almost certain he could see Antero's mouth and jaw moving and assumed this was a private moment.

Ilmari heard the occasional, distant sounds of traffic, one particularly loud sound, like a car accelerating, then more silence. He was cold but at the same time he was grateful for the calm, windless evening. He looked at Antero again. Yes, he was talking; his lips were moving. Ilmari instinctively looked away and tried to warm himself with little movements, shifting his body weight from one leg to the other, giving his arms the occasional shake.

Time passed.

Then Antero turned, walked back using the footprints he had already created in the snow and returned to the narrow pathway where Ilmari was waiting. Antero stood beside him but didn't look at him, keeping his eyes fixed on the gravestone instead.

'He did his best,' said Antero.

Ilmari didn't know what to say, so he said nothing.

'And we've got Niilo Kuikka to thank that the van is still running,' Antero continued. 'Our van and probably many other people's vans too. I wish I'd asked him why cars were always so damn important to him, especially the kind of cars that need constant care and maintenance. I hated him, and those cars.' Antero held a short pause. 'But I don't hate them anymore,' he said.

He paused again, then continued:

'It's good that we came here. Thank you.'

'You're welcome,' said Ilmari.

They stood on the spot. Antero looked like he was about to continue his monologue to the gravestone.

'There are so many sides to us,' he said.

'I've noticed,' said Ilmari.

'But why do we always show our worst sides to those nearest to us?'

'I don't know,' said Ilmari with a shrug, partly because he wanted to show that he didn't know much about life either, partly because he was freezing cold. At the same moment, he noticed that Antero was now standing slightly further away from him, nearer to the wall of dark trees through which they had arrived at the grave. Ilmari hadn't noticed him move.

'I remember thinking I'd never do anything like my father,' said Antero. 'That I'd never make decisions that left other people high and dry. Then I went and did it anyway. Just like my father.'

Ilmari said nothing. Then, either due to Antero's words or the direction he was looking or something else, his eyes moved, and he looked at Niilo Kuikka's final resting place once again.

Nothing about it had changed. It was a dark, snow-covered grave that looked like nobody had visited it for a long time. Ilmari turned and was about to suggest that they go back to the van, but there was no need. Antero was gone. Ilmari was alone.

The image returned like a punch in the gut.

Ilmari had seen Antero talking on the telephone at the petrol station.

He remembered his question, and he remembered Antero's answer too. Now he realised that Antero couldn't have been calling his relatives, because where Antero's relatives lived, nobody would answer the phone.

Ilmari walked off, cursing himself as he went.

Running at full speed was out of the question; he still had to find a firm footing for each step. He hurried along the same dark pathway between the two lamps. As he approached the main path, he wondered how Antero could have got so far ahead of him so quickly. How long had Ilmari stood staring at the frost-covered headstone? He cursed again, more to himself than anything, and might have done so out loud. He was reaching the end of the most arduous stretch of the trail, which joined the illuminated and recently ploughed main pathway, and he was just about to break into a run when the light was suddenly obscured.

Ilmari was already a little off balance. He saw the figure lunge at him, but he couldn't dodge to the side. To his left was a freshly dug grave, and the figure whom Ilmari now recognised both by sight and smell, was hurtling towards him from the right. Before he knew it, the air was knocked from his lungs and his feet were no longer touching the ground, and he knew where he was heading.

The Outlaw was taking him to an early grave.

33

Anneli Kukkorinne had made her decision. She had a gun, and that meant two things. She could get the sofa back by herself, without help from anyone else. But before that, she would sort out the problem sitting right next to her.

They were sitting in the truck near a bridge on the only road leading to Kilpisjärvi, the open landscape allowing them to see any potential new arrivals one and a half kilometres in all directions. Right now, the road was empty.

What's more, Erkki had *finally* listened to her and agreed not to smoke in the cab of the truck.

Erkki slipped a cigarette between his lips, buttoned up his coat and opened the driver's door. Anneli quickly said she could do with some fresh air too, and they both jumped out of the cab and into the chilled, moonlit evening. Anneli stopped as soon as her feet touched the ground, pushed her hands into her jacket pocket, took a firm grip on the handle of her gun and walked around the truck.

She had thought this through many times.

And enough was enough.

She didn't like the thought of what she was about to do, but she couldn't see any other options. Erkki was either planning to betray her, or the entire cause, which, right now, were one and the same thing. And when she asked herself what Lenin or Stalin would have done in a similar situation – once they had identified any traitors, class enemies or other clandestine capitalists – this lent her plan and its implementation a certain historical jus-tification. Of course, it wasn't particularly nice or pleasant to get rid of people once and for all, people you had spent a lot of time with, but the plan had to be put into effect, if the greater good required it. Lenin and Stalin had known this. And besides, which of them would get their own mausoleum: a jovial clown with a penchant for sausages who routinely failed at everything he tried to accomplish, or someone who put the revolution above everything else and did not settle for compromises?

Erkki was standing with his back to her, smoking his filterless cigarette, looking in the direction they had come from. The smoke rose around his head and dispersed into the air. Anneli looked in both directions once more, though she knew it was pointless. Bathed in moonlight, the road was just as empty as a moment ago. She took the pistol from her pocket, held it against her thigh, took a few determined steps towards Erkki.

Anneli knew – and she had known all along – that she wouldn't be able to shoot Erkki, but there were other ways to use a gun. The pistol was hard and heavy, and it fitted her hand beautifully. It was just the right size. She could use it to hit him, to knock him out. The minus-twenty temperatures would take care of the rest. That didn't feel very easy either. No. But there were no other options.

Another three steps, and Anneli would be one hundred percent certain of success. She raised her right hand, concentrated all her strength into her arm. She took another step, and had just caught the smell of tobacco, when she heard Erkki say:

'You know what I like most?'

The question took Anneli completely by surprise. Both the question and the way it was asked. It messed with her thoughts, messed up her steps, and she had to stop. At the same time, she realised that she was too far behind him. She quickly slipped the pistol behind her back, which was lucky, because Erkki turned, not quite in her direction but enough that he could see what she was doing and where she was standing.

'What's that?' she asked – or heard herself asking.

'Our assignments,' said Erkki. 'Spending time together. Not in a romantic way, mind.'

'I wasn't thinking anything romantic,' said Anneli.

'Like I said, Airi threw me out two years ago. My sister's nice, but she doesn't half talk a lot. But you and me ... we just talk when we need to.'

'That's true,' said Anneli.

'Don't get me wrong, I like my sister,' said Erkki. 'A lot. But all that prattle makes me feel a bit lonely. I feel lonely everywhere, really. But then again...'

Erkki swallowed loudly, sucked what was left of his cigarette.

'I might as well say it out loud,' he said, now turning to face her directly. 'But I don't feel lonely when I'm with you.'

His eyes looked moist, and at first Anneli wanted to believe that it was because of the freezing weather and the cigarette smoke and everything else, but then, against her will and unexpectedly, she realised that her own eyes felt moist too. It had happened without her volition, but at the same time it felt completely logical. Which made the matter even stranger and more alarming. What was happening to her? she wondered again, mentally shouting at herself. She suddenly realised that she couldn't lift her arm. Not even if she had wanted to. And that wasn't the only part of her that was now beyond her control. She felt like a mere passenger carried forwards by an unseen force, hurtling towards...

'Friendship,' said Erkki. 'I suppose that's what I'm trying to describe ... Something like that ... I think of you as a friend.'

Anneli tried to think of Lenin, then Stalin, then the swift, summary liquidation of the enemy. But the thought kept slipping out of reach. She felt tears in her eyes and, in a strange way, imagined all their shared assignments flowing through her mind as images and memories. She and Erkki, all these years, from one adventure to the next. It wasn't romantic, of course, nothing like that, but it was undeniably powerful.

'A friend,' she said. She tried to make it sound like a question, but neither the word nor her voice would yield. And so, she sounded like she was affirming what Erkki had just said. And judging by his nod, this was exactly how he took it too: as encouragement.

'I know I haven't been myself lately,' he said. 'Far from it. And I know I've been acting strangely. I've been having trouble getting a grip on things. I imagine you noticed something was up.'

'Little things,' Anneli nodded.

'That's what I was worried about,' Erkki sighed. 'And naturally you've come to all kinds of conclusions.'

Anneli looked up towards the fells standing in front of them like great, soft-white waves. Earth and space in the same location. Both near and far. She tried to fight against the feeling one last time, but it was too powerful, and she had to give up once and for all.

'I have been thinking ... this and that.'

'Right,' said Erkki. 'I'm sure it's worrying when someone ... you know. Especially as our mission is so important, but I haven't been able to give it my full attention. My thoughts have been all over the place, and I've probably said the weirdest things. But it's all because of this ... inner struggle. I'm sorry.'

Anneli raised her shoulders. Naturally, she raised her right shoulder a little more carefully; she wasn't sure whether she still had a firm grip on the pistol.

'It's okay,' she said. 'This is ... good to know.'

She meant it. Now she had an explanation. She knew something that she hadn't known only a few moments earlier. Erkki was going through a difficult patch. Anneli had heard about people having a mid-life crisis, but maybe people well past middle age could have crises too. Maybe we never stopped having crises, no matter how grey our hair or how strange our behaviour – like Erkki. She felt a kind of relief that she'd never felt before. Where there had been suspicion and doubt, now there was something else.

'I don't remember ever saying something like this to anyone before,' said Erkki.

'I won't tell anybody,' said Anneli.

'I know,' said Erkki. 'And it feels good. It feels like I'm not alone anymore.'

'You're not alone,' said Anneli, and the words came from somewhere deep inside her, and they had escaped her mouth before she could shape them into something else. At the same time, her thoughts wandered elsewhere, somewhere she hadn't allowed them for a long time. She knew the truth about herself. She had known it for years. She'd thought she deserved this truth, that it was part of what she was doing and trying to achieve.

'I know what it feels like,' she said. 'To be lonely.'

Erkki looked at her without speaking. Then said:

'You're my best friend.'

Anneli said nothing. She didn't know how long they stood in silence before moving again. Each of them took a step forwards, threw their arms around the other, and they held each other tight. Anneli felt a tear running down her cheek, tickling her skin. Because she was taller than Erkki and her arms longer than his, she kept her arms up and was able to move them freely. And so she checked she had a good grip on the handle of the gun, mustered all her strength, then raised her hand and wiped her cheek with the barrel of the pistol.

34

The grave was cold and hard. Ilmari hit his head against its frozen bottom as the Outlaw slammed down on top of him like a tonne of alcohol-smelling cement, winding him. The pain in his back seemed to erase what little was left of his consciousness. Ilmari provided the Outlaw with a soft landing, and presumably that was why he was able to start battering Ilmari right away. The Outlaw hit him wherever he could reach; Ilmari protected himself as best he could. The mittens flew from his hands, his woolly hat disappeared. However, the cramped conditions in the grave gave Ilmari an advantage. The Outlaw couldn't move entirely freely, and Ilmari was able to block many of his blows. He thought that, as long as the situation continued like this, he might have a chance of changing the course of events. He didn't quite know how yet, but if he had time, he might be able to come up with...

The Outlaw seemed to realise the same thing at exactly the same moment.

He stopped throwing punches, let go of Ilmari and jumped backwards. Then he leapt to his feet and brought his right boot down on Ilmari's left knee. Ilmari knew he was the underdog in this fight. He couldn't even try to stand up; the Outlaw was pressing his knee so hard that it was nearly crushed against the rock-solid bottom of the frozen grave.

Lying in the grave, looking directly up, Ilmari saw a yellowish glow, the tips of spruce branches, the black sky and the stars somewhere unfathomably far away. The thought of the black piano flashed through his mind, his daughter's fingers on its white keys. He no longer cursed himself, but he reached the conclusion that trusting Antero had been the worst decision of his life. And the fact that that mistake had resulted in a dozen smaller mistakes felt like ample punishment. He was only half conscious, but he knew that the Outlaw would soon do something nasty, something terminal. He tried to see whether there was anything he could reach with his hands, but all he could see in the pitch-dark grave was the frozen, black earth. He scraped the sandy pit beneath him looking for a rock to throw, but only managed to get some grains of sand stuck under his nails.

'Have you been laughing at me?'

At first, Ilmari didn't understand that someone was speaking, let alone that the voice belonged to the Outlaw. Then he managed to focus and saw that the Outlaw was standing right above him. Despite the dim, Ilmari could tell that his face was pummelled, covered in bashes and bruises. His eyes were like dark holes in a rugged cliff.

'What?' asked Ilmari, because he was sure he had heard wrong.

'Have you – you and your friend – been laughing at me?'

Given the circumstances, the question felt barking mad, but it still took Ilmari by surprise. This might give him a little more time. He strained to fill his lungs with air and to make his mouth form words.

'Why would we be laughing at you?' he asked.

'You know.'

Naturally, Ilmari didn't know what to say to that, but he had to humour this curious and obviously life-threatening man for as long as possible.

'Because we've got the sofa,' Ilmari said. 'And you want it.'

'I'll get the sofa,' said the man. 'That won't be a problem.'

'Then what *is* the problem?'

'Smug dickheads like you, who think they're better than everybody else.'

'I don't think I—'

'Always running around with your bum chum.'

'We're not—'

'And where is he now?' asked the man. 'Where friends usually are. He's fucked off. That's friends for you. I don't need friends. You can beg me all you like, I'm not going to be your friend.'

'You don't have to—'

'Shut it.'

Ilmari said nothing further, but continued scraping the ground with his nails, trying to gather as much sand in his fist as possible.

'People always let you down,' the man continued. 'Every sodding time. Sooner or later. No matter what you do, everyone turns against you in the end. You can't trust anybody ... But you know who you *can* trust?'

Ilmari's fist was nearly full.

'I don't think I do,' he said.

'Yourself,' said the man. 'You can only ever trust yourself. I trust myself. I'll survive by myself.'

'That's one way of—'

'It's the only way,' said the man, and Ilmari could hear from his voice that he was whipping himself up into a rage. 'Because otherwise you get yourself tricked, fooled, scammed, conned. And it'll serve you two right. So, you tossers can keep on plaiting each other's hair. I'm going to kill you all.'

Ilmari gathered some last bits of earth into his fist. It was almost full.

'The sofa,' he said. 'If you want it, you're going to need the van—'

'I'll get the sofa and I'll get the van,' the Outlaw bellowed. 'But there's one thing you need to understand first.'

'And what's that?' Ilmari asked, but didn't wait for an answer. 'The keys are in my trouser pocket, and I can't move my hands.'

The question and this new information had the desired effect. The man's fury grew even further, but he seemed a little confused too. His mouth opened, perhaps to shout another obscenity, but instead he bowed over and reached his right hand towards Ilmari's left-hand trouser pocket. Ilmari waited until the man's face was as close as possible. He gathered his strength, tried to aim as carefully as he could, then raised his hand and opened his fist at just the right moment. The sand flew right into the man's eyes. He sprung backwards, raised his hands to his face and started wiping his eyes.

'I'll drive my thumbs into your fucking eye sockets,' the man shouted. 'Fucking fake friend ... I'll dig your brain out of your ... then we'll see whose eyes are stinging ... you fucking ... friend...'

Ilmari tried to get up, only to realise that the Outlaw had stopped rubbing his eyes. The sand had bought him some time, but not enough. The Outlaw returned his boot to Ilmari's knee, and this time with a kick to ram the point home. Ilmari was winded again. The Outlaw pulled something out of the pocket of his large coat. A bottle of beer. He pulled off the lid with his teeth, spat it out, and downed the foaming contents in seconds. Then he turned the bottle in his hand, grabbed it by the neck and swung it against the grave's frozen wall. The glass gave a clink and smashed, leaving a sharp, jagged-edged weapon in his hand. The man burped, then returned his attention to Ilmari. He could see the Outlaw's eyes now, and he felt he was staring into an even deeper grave than the one in which he was currently lying.

'Real friendship,' said the man, his voice now sounding like it was coming from somewhere other than a human mouth, 'isn't just about words, it's about deeds...'

The Outlaw couldn't see what Ilmari saw as he looked up.

Something was flying through the yellow dusk, between the black sky and the distant stars, like a hawk homing in on its prey or a falling star moving in a straight line. Its journey stopped abruptly and a little surprisingly at the Outlaw's head, and the impact sounded like a church bell or a large triangle wrapped in a blanket. The Outlaw remained upright, but now his movements slowed. He removed his foot from Ilmari's knee and turned as if trying to move through a pool of quicksand. And this was why he was unable to dodge the next hawk attack, the next falling star. If it were possible, this clank was even louder, like a thousand doorbells ringing inside the same house. The Outlaw was still upright. He touched his forehead at the spot where the second blow had struck him. Then he raised his foot as if he intended to climb out of the grave, but he could not. The bells rang a third time. The Outlaw's leg remained in mid-air – he was standing in the grave on one leg and looked like he was performing a particularly convoluted dance routine in a uniquely awkward place. Then he began to topple, and though Ilmari saw the man falling towards him, all he could do was prepare to cushion his fall.

Ilmari found himself lying in the grave with the unconscious Outlaw in his arms. He heard something, then saw Antero's face far above him, surrounded by the stars.

'Took a while to find his shovel,' said Antero.

35

'It's a question of trust,' said Antero from the other side of the van, as Ilmari opened the driver's door. 'That's what friendship's about. I had to do what I thought was right. I saw someone approaching, and I made a quick decision. There wasn't time to draw up a plan, let alone discuss it with you. I had to act. I assumed you'd understand.'

Ilmari didn't answer. He hadn't said a word since climbing out of the grave. Perhaps Antero had concluded something from his expression, and perhaps that had affected him, making him more talkative than usual.

Ilmari's fingers were sore, both from scraping the sand and from the cold. He didn't know where his mittens had ended up during all the wrestling. They weren't underneath the Outlaw, nor anywhere else in the pit. Ilmari didn't have the strength to think or care about his mittens. He climbed into the van, leant over to open the passenger door for Antero, but his hand stopped just before it reached the lock. Ilmari recalled what he had thought when the Outlaw attacked him. He saw Antero's face, the glow of the streetlamps rendering it asymmetrical, at once pallid and cast in shadow. Ilmari thought for a moment, then lifted the lock, and Antero opened the door and clambered into his seat. Ilmari switched on the engine, reversed out to the road, stopped the van in the middle of the empty carriageway, put it into gear and drove off.

'No disrespect,' Antero continued as they approached the centre of Rovaniemi for the second time, 'but I knew that if I'd told you there was someone lurking in the trees, someone who might be armed, you'd start asking questions and, in the worst-case scenario, you wouldn't agree to my plan. We would have lost the element of surprise. And that's what saved us. The fact that I was able to catch him completely off-guard.'

Ilmari remained silent. He looked around. The evening in Rovaniemi was dark and distinctly deserted. He saw a few tourists doddering along the pavements in ski boots, looking like they had just learnt to walk but hadn't quite got the hang of it. Then Ilmari found what he was looking for. He steered the van into the car park, guided them into a parking space and switched off the engine.

Antero looked first right, then left, then straight ahead and eventually asked:

'Why are we at the railway station?'

Ilmari looked at him, felt a searing pain in his lower back and left shoulder and a dull ache all over his face. He knew that he looked like he'd just had a brawl in an icy grave. He wasn't sure what he was doing, but he thought Antero appeared on edge.

'Remember when we had those schnitzels?' he asked.

'Of course,' said Antero. 'They were delicious.'

'Delicious?'

'And plenty of chips,' Antero added. 'For once.'

'You clearly remember everything,' said Ilmari. 'That's great. So can you tell me which of your Rovaniemi relatives you telephoned from the petrol station?'

Antero was taken aback. It was the first time Ilmari had seen him look even remotely bewildered.

'Telephoned?'

'Yes,' said Ilmari. 'I saw you at the petrol station. I went to get some coffee, and I saw you at the phone booth, holding the handset to your ear. I don't think anyone at that graveyard is in the habit of answering the phone.'

Antero's bewilderment was gone, but now he tried to avoid

Ilmari's stare, looked over towards the station building and said nothing.

'That's quite a lot of coincidences,' Ilmari continued. 'First the call, then the touching monologue at the graveside to distract me, then your disappearing act, and then, as if by magic, that madman turns up and knocks the living daylights out of me.'

'I don't know exactly how he found us,' said Antero, his voice now quieter, almost hushed. 'But with my experience of the Legion, I can tell you that spotting someone in open terrain isn't very hard. We're driving an ancient light-blue British van and following a route that every man and his dog seems to know. You'd have to be a dismal assassin not to find us. And you can say what you like about that guy, he's nothing if not resourceful.'

'Are you telling me you didn't telephone anybody?' asked Ilmari.

Antero shook his head, and Ilmari heard him give a sigh. 'Of course not,' said Antero, turning to face Ilmari. 'I'm just saying I didn't phone anyone who might have threatened us in any way.'

'Then you can tell me who you phoned.'

'No, I can't,' said Antero.

'Why not?'

'Because I made a promise.'

Ilmari was silent for a moment.

'You're not leaving me many options,' he said.

'I suppose that's why we're here,' said Antero. It wasn't a question.

Ilmari looked away from Antero, stared at the railway station and the grey-blue train pulling up to the platform.

'You'll be in Helsinki by morning,' he said.

Antero didn't answer at first. Then he moved his hand, opened the door.

'I'll leave the shovel and the shotgun,' he said. 'They might come in handy, especially the shovel. You can dig your own grave in peace and quiet, with nobody there to disturb you.'

'At least I won't be in for any surprises,' said Ilmari.

'You know what your problem is?'

'I was just trying to tell you.'

'When someone offers you something on a silver platter,' said Antero, 'you turn the other way.'

'What's that supposed to mean?'

'Why don't you ask your ex-wife?' said Antero.

Ilmari was about to say something but stopped himself. Besides, he was in a hurry: the sofa and the man inside it were expected in Kilpisjärvi.

Antero climbed out of the van, took his bag from the footwell and closed the door. He didn't look at Ilmari. He turned and threw the bag over his shoulder, and began walking towards the station house.

Ilmari sat in the van looking at the train waiting at the platform. He couldn't see Antero anymore. He put the van in gear, drove out of the car park and headed north.

36

Anneli Kukkorinne and Erkki Liljalampi were standing next to each other and looking in the same direction. Anneli wondered whether the stars were brighter and the moon even fuller than a few hours ago when she had considered streamlining their assignment by getting rid of Erkki. She hadn't done so, and now every star was shining, like the lights of a million aircraft all flying home. And she and Erkki were on board, flying home too. Both of them, together.

But right now, they were observing the van, following its trajectory.

The van was still far away, and there was no way of being absolutely certain about its colour, but they both knew it was the right van. They stood on the spot a moment longer, then Erkki turned, walked back to the truck, climbed into the cab and switched on the engine, leaving the lights off. At the same time, Anneli walked to the other side of the bridge, jumped off the road and climbed into the foxhole she had dug herself in the snow. She could see the road, but someone driving past wouldn't be able to see her. She checked that the gun was still in her pocket.

Erkki and the truck were hidden behind a cluster of frost-covered birches, their tangled branches black, so that only the upper part of the cab remained visible, and even that only at close range. From a distance, it was impossible to distinguish the truck from the trees. They watched the van approaching, well aware that they had a head start, as well as plans A and B. Anneli hadn't wanted to put all her eggs in the same basket. She had justified this with reference to their recent, shared, experiences, and Erkki had agreed right away. That felt good too. In fact, everything seemed to have changed for the better.

Anneli gripped the pistol. She could already hear the van's engine. She listened to it, noted that the sound was changing as it approached the bridge. At first, she'd assumed that the puttering sound must be because the van was travelling through the hilly, snow-covered terrain. But when it came closer to the bridge, she thought there must be something wrong with its engine. Then, as it finally reached the bridge, she realised that the van had simply run out of fuel. There was no mistaking the sound. The van spluttered, sounding more bronchial by the minute, then it continued to slow, until it finally slid a short distance and came to a halt right before the bridge.

They had parked the truck across the road, their plan being to stop the van on the bridge, then, a second or two later, Anneli would appear in the van's rearview mirror with her pistol, blocking it from behind. Of course, the van might still have tried to reverse – there wasn't enough room on the narrow bridge for it to turn around, and certainly not very quickly – but the battle between an old van in reverse and a new truck moving forward would soon end in the truck's favour.

Anneli looked towards the other end of the bridge. Erkki couldn't have heard that the van had run out of petrol. Both plans A and B featured him blocking the road across the bridge with the truck, but neither plan accounted for the van stopping *before* the bridge.

Unperturbed, Anneli sprang into action. She dashed out into the road, as fast as she could, approached the van, reached the back end, then moved on until she was beside the passenger window. She peeked inside and saw an empty seat. She ducked her head and saw the driver's hands on the steering wheel. She made a quick decision: she wrenched the door open, aimed the gun inside and glanced into the cargo space at the back of the van. The van was carrying only one man and one sofa.

'Run out of petrol,' said the driver.

Anneli examined him more closely. He looked like he'd been through the wars, as though he had dug a pit in the frozen earth then battered his head against the ground.

Anneli pointed the pistol at him. 'Where's your accomplice?'

'We...' he hesitated, 'had a difference of opinion.'

Anneli considered this answer for a moment, and she thought that perhaps she understood him. What's more, he sounded sincere, just as he had when he told her he had run out of fuel.

'Out,' she said.

The driver moved slowly, and Anneli could see that it was mostly because he was in pain. He seemed to be avoiding using his left arm. He had to swing himself out of the seat and reach his right arm across himself to open the door. Eventually, however, he got out and stood on the other side of the road. Anneli walked around the front of the van, keeping her pistol aimed at the driver all the while.

And there they finally were. All in the same place at the same time, everything under Anneli's control.

Man, van and sofa.

Though their plan hadn't worked out perfectly, the results were the same.

Anneli felt a sense of relief, as well as some contentment – a feeling that grew with every passing moment and was well on its way to turning into triumph. She waved to Erkki. This was the signal he had been waiting for, and the truck's engine roared into life. He pulled the truck up next to the van, switched off the engine and hopped down from the cab. Anneli kept her eyes on the driver, though this felt unnecessary. Aside from his physical constraints, he looked like he had given up once and for all. But they still needed him, for a moment at least. Which meant they had to keep him alive.

'We're working for the common good,' said Anneli.

'Pardon?' said the driver, who seemed lost in thought.

'So, you can help us move the sofa from the van into the truck.'

'Help you? You're stealing my sofa, and I'm supposed to help you?'

'We're not stealing it,' said Anneli. 'It will become our shared property. Just like everything else one day. The sofa is a means to that noble end.'

The driver stared at her. 'It's a dangerous sofa,' he said.

'I know what you mean,' said Anneli. 'But not anymore. We'll make sure of that. We come in peace.'

'You're holding a pistol.'

'I mean, in a broader sense.'

'Of course.'

Erkki had walked past them and opened the back of the van. Anneli heard the screech of the old metal hinges. Then she heard Erkki's voice.

'It's here,' he said. 'And it's a hundred times finer than I'd thought.'

Anneli flicked her gun, and the driver moved. They walked round to the back of the van. Anneli peered inside. In the moonlight, the sofa glowed in a way that suggested an innate grandeur and, of course, value. It was so beautiful that Anneli had to take deep breaths and concentrate before she was able to speak again. She told Erkki to get to work.

Erkki and the van's driver agreed on how to lift the sofa, eventually found a suitable way to distribute the weight, and lifted it out of the van and onto the road. Once on the road, they tightened their gloves, resumed their respective positions and set off carrying the sofa. Despite his slender frame, the driver, whose clothes suggested he'd recently been in a mud-wrestling match, was surprisingly strong and agile, even when most of the weight on his end rested on his right arm.

'Does your work involve lots of physical labour?' asked Anneli once the sofa had been positioned behind the truck in front of the tail lift, ready for the final push.

'I work with heavy parcels at the sorting office,' he said.

'Then you're one of us,' said Anneli. 'We're fighting the same fight.'

'Your work involves hard physical labour too?'

'Not exactly,' said Anneli. 'But I spend a lot of time thinking about it.'

The driver regarded her but said nothing. Erkki explained how the sofa would be lifted into the back of the truck. The plan required Anneli climbing onto the tail lift to help guide the sofa into place. Erkki and the driver lifted the sofa and pushed it towards the edge of the lift. This required all three of them, because the sofa was heavy. Once the sofa's first two legs had been placed on the lift, the task became much easier. Anneli pulled the sofa; the men pushed it. The sofa's legs gave a long, low rattle as they scraped across the platform, and the sound seemed all the louder in the otherwise still and quiet night. Finally, the men gave a firm shove, and Anneli managed to haul the sofa into the middle of the platform.

She walked around the sofa, returned to the edge of the platform and was about to tell Erkki that they still had to tie up the driver by the hands and feet and lock him in the van, after which they could knock the van off the road and return to Helsinki.

This was her plan. But she said none of it out loud.

What she heard seemed to have no connection to anything

that had already happened, and this in turn meant that her reactions were slower. Something ripped or came loose and fell on the platform behind her, followed by a thud, which itself was followed by two thumps. Not thumps, necessarily, but steps. She thought of the pistol she had momentarily put down – who could hold a gun *and* move a sofa at the same time? – and suddenly she couldn't see it anywhere.

She looked up, saw the stars, the soft flanks of the fells.

She didn't turn. She knew it was too late.

37

Ilmari Nieminen had left Rovaniemi behind him without looking back. In the train-station car park, he had wanted to tell Antero he was wrong. But for some reason, even in the heat of the moment, it hadn't felt like the most compelling rebuttal. And after five kilometres of upset and disappointment, then another five of self-reflection and considerably more honest consideration, he knew why. Antero hadn't been wrong; he had been right. Ilmari had known it, but in the moment, he hadn't known what he could or should have done about it.

Then he did know.

He had turned the van and found Antero Kuikka still sitting in the waiting room at the railway station. Ilmari got straight to the point and thanked him for saving his life. Antero had asked whether this was an apology, and Ilmari had sat down and said yes, yes it was, and the first of many, as the person who deserved the next apology was Tuulikki because, on more than one occasion, Ilmari had been wrong, both when it came to things and people. They had sat down opposite each other, then Antero had put down his bottle of lemonade, picked up his bag and said that he too had had time to think things through.

And now Antero was standing behind a woman in a balaclava on the hydraulic lift of a large truck, with the black barrel of a shotgun in his hand, the removable back of the sofa at his feet and encouraging all those present to remain calm.

'Off the platform,' Antero instructed the woman as Ilmari took a few steps backwards and to the side, leaving the balaclava-clad robbers in the line of fire. Ilmari couldn't see the pistol in the woman's hand anymore. It wasn't on the platform either; the moonlight would have revealed it. And the robber who had helped Ilmari lift the sofa couldn't have taken it either, because he had been carrying the other end of the sofa and hadn't gone anywhere near the edge of the lift. Ilmari didn't have time to think about the matter any further. Antero and the woman had stepped down from the lift.

'Balaclavas off,' said Antero. 'And, if I may, sooner rather than later.'

'Why?' asked the female robber.

'So we can get to know one another,' said Ilmari.

The robbers turned, looked at Ilmari, then turned again and looked at Antero, who was still holding the shotgun. Then, after briefly considering their options, they removed their balaclavas almost in sync. The silver-haired, stony-faced man looked more disappointed than surprised or angered. The brunette with the ruddy cheeks and a fiery passion in her eyes asked:

'What now? Are you going to kill us?'

'Not right now,' said Ilmari. 'But we want to get a good look at your faces, in case we need to describe them later on.'

The robbers remained silent.

'Let's walk back to the van,' said Antero. 'You can help us.'

The robbers didn't seem to understand the instruction. Antero repeated it. The robbers started moving. Antero and Ilmari let them walk three metres ahead, giving themselves enough distance to dodge a potential attack and ensuring that the shotgun could hit either of them at any time. They arrived at the van, and Ilmari dropped to his knees, then rolled under the car on his back. He worked as quickly as the cold and his stiff fingers would permit, untying the knots and detaching the straps, and the body of the crime boss, wrapped in a blanket, dropped onto the snowy surface of the road. Still under the van, Ilmari rolled onto his side and, using both his hands and feet, pushed the body from under the van – it slid excellently across the ice – then got out himself and told the robbers to get to work.

'You've already killed someone?' asked the silver-haired man.

Ilmari shook his head. 'This one was on the house,' he said.

The robbers glanced at each other; they clearly had no idea what any of this was about. Probably for the best, thought Ilmari. Antero waved the shotgun, signalling for the robbers to hurry up. The robbers grabbed the rolled-up blanket, took a firm grip and carried it towards the truck. It was hard going. Eventually, they hoisted the body onto the truck's hydraulic lift and positioned it beside the sofa. The robbers stood in front of Antero's shotgun and tried to catch their breath.

'What now?' asked the woman.

'Nothing,' said Antero. 'Just remember that we'll remember.'

The robbers glanced at each other. They looked both worried and at a loss.

'You can go,' said Ilmari. 'The van is yours. Take it.'

The robbers stood on the spot a few seconds longer. The woman was the first to turn, taking a few cautious steps away from them. The silver-haired man plucked up courage, then he too turned and began to walk away. Ilmari watched them go. The robbers gathered speed the further away they got. They crossed the bridge and started running. After reaching the van, they opened the doors and sat down inside, and Ilmari could hear the man in the driver's seat trying to start the engine. Naturally, he couldn't. It was out of fuel.

38

The world was a piece of shit, and the people in it nothing but slimy knobheads. Otto Puolanka couldn't see ahead, but he kept the accelerator rammed against the floor, nonetheless. His eyes seemed to be covered in everything that had been building up over the last few days: sand from the graveyard, windscreen fluid from the Lada, snow, blood, tears. He calculated that he would reach Kilpisjärvi in two hours and promised himself that, once he got there, he would kill everybody. Then he would drive back to Helsinki and kill everybody there too. Every last couch potato. Speaking of couches, there was one in particular that needed burning.

Luckily, this road was made for driving. Long, straight stretches of tarmac, only gentle bends. It was a relief. The pain in his leg had reached new heights now that the anaesthetic had started to wear off. The Saab went uphill for around a kilometre at a steady pace, slowing the closer it got to the ridge. Before reaching the top, Otto again had to rub his eyes. This helped, but only for a few seconds. Then the stinging and the itching returned, now more painful, more bothersome.

Once the car reached the top of the hill – or was this a fell? Otto neither knew nor cared – he had to slow down slightly. His eyes were burning so much now, he couldn't see anything at all. He let out a roar and tried to steer the car to the side of the road. This didn't work out quite the way he had planned. He braked too hard, the tyres locked, the car began to slide and eventually came to a halt sideways across the road. Otto flung the door open, ran to the verge and started rubbing cold snow into his eyes, howling all the while. He rubbed his whole face with snow, bellowing at the top of his voice that he hated every human being who'd ever existed and every sofa ever built; he hated them like he hated boils on his backside, like he hated herpes – and added that he knew what he was talking about on both accounts. The snow helped, he dried his eyes and could see in front of him again. He turned, looked the way he was heading.

He hadn't realised how bright the moon was, how the snow reflected and amplified it. The silvery disc was like a floodlight in the undulating, nocturnal landscape. And like a floodlight, it illuminated things further away too, things further down in the valley – including a tiny spot whose shape and form started to come into focus the more he squinted at it. Eventually, the spot took on a faint colour too, and Otto knew that he had found what he had been looking for. A light-blue van. On the bridge up ahead.

Anneli Kukkorinne had had enough. Of sitting in this cold, smoke-filled van, of Erkki's silence, of blankly staring ahead, of tasting the bitterness of defeat. She opened the door, climbed out. She wanted to stretch her legs, warm herself up. She closed the door behind her – it made no difference to the temperature, but she knew Erkki would appreciate it – and took a few steps.

It was a bright night, almost as bright as day, but in a different way, like walking through an X-ray image. Once her legs began to come back to life, she took longer strides. The snow crunched underfoot; the echo returned to her from afar. She reached the side of the bridge where their truck had been stolen. Erkki had been here earlier to look for his cigarettes, which must have fallen out of his pocket while they were being hijacked, and now he was running low. Anneli couldn't see any cigarettes or anything else. Just the spot where she had been tricked. The very thought of it was infuriating.

She turned and was starting to walk back to the van when, in hope of salvation either in the form of fuel or a lift, she glanced back the way they had come. She stopped, something flickered inside her, then she felt an ice-cold bolt of lightning run from her head to her toes.

With the light of the moon behind it, the vehicle was like half an egg cut from a sheet of cardboard. It was far away, but there was no mistaking its shape. Anneli couldn't think of any reason why there was a Saab 96 sideways across the road at the top of the fell, but there it was. The car seemed to have come to a halt. Anneli knew who was driving it, and that its appearance on the horizon was no coincidence. The only coincidence was that she had seen it. She tried to divine something from the car's position. And just when she wondered whether the car might have driven off the road and been damaged and the driver perhaps injured, it started moving. Its profile changed, its front lights now aiming forwards, right at her.

The Saab was heading towards them.

Anneli ran, shouting to Erkki that he needed to get out of the van. She saw him open the driver's door – she didn't know why he had been sitting at the wheel all this time, as if pretending to play dodgems. He moved slowly, stepping out of the cab as if from a long, satisfying sleep. Finally, he looked back in the direction from which they had come.

Anneli stopped next to him. Her heart was racing. She was furious in so many ways that she couldn't keep track of them all.

'If I still had the pistol,' she said, 'I'd shoot that creep. It's the damn cowboy. That's what happens when you watch too many films. It should be—'

'Violence is never the answer,' said Erkki.

At first, Anneli didn't understand what she'd just heard, but then it all made sense. As she watched and now heard the Saab approaching, she realised that Erkki was old. That was it. He was just old, and maybe that was why he didn't understand the gravity of their situation.

The road down into the valley curved round a corner, and the Saab momentarily disappeared behind the trees. Once it was out of sight, Erkki took Anneli by surprise. He gripped her arm, led her round to the van's back doors, which were still standing wide open, and practically lifted her inside. He climbed in after her and pulled the doors shut behind him. Everything happened so quickly and suddenly that Anneli had no time to ask what was going on, let alone resist. Now, huddling behind Erkki in the back of the van, she saw that he had left the doors ajar. They watched the Saab reappear from behind the trees, listened to its angry engine.

'What now?' she asked.

'We'll play it by ear,' said Erkki.

Anneli wasn't quite sure what he meant, but at the same time she had to admit that hiding in the back had given them a few crucial extra seconds compared to waiting for the new arrival in the middle of the road. She just didn't know what they would do with those extra seconds. Then she heard the Saab, and a moment later, the music. She instantly recognised it. The same song had been playing last time too, when she had run the cowboy over.

Otto Puolanka was singing along, slapping his hands against the steering wheel in rhythm. Now that he could see clearly again, he noticed that his thoughts had cleared too. He wasn't going to waste time trying to get people to understand things anymore. It was impossible; he knew that now. People only listened to themselves, only believed their own stupid conclusions, closed their ears to all common sense. In looking for consensus, for mutual understanding, he had made a mistake, one that he now planned to correct. He would start correcting it here. He would kill them all and wouldn't speak to anyone. Even accidentally.

'Eye of the Tiger'.

Otto braked suddenly and brought the Saab to a halt about ten metres from the van. He picked up the billhook he had bought at the petrol station, wrapped his fingers around the handle, making sure he had a firm grip. He stepped out of the car, looked around. The landscape was still there, no movement in sight. Just miles and miles of Lapland. You can keep your fucking reindeer, stick them where the sun don't shine, he thought. He tapped the billhook against his leg in time with the music and felt that familiar, exhilarating feeling. He was being watched. He knew it. He always knew when he was being observed; it was one of his predator's skills.

Speaking of prey...

The movement was tiny, imperceptible, but Otto noticed it. The van's back doors were ajar, not closed after all, though that's what it had looked like at first glance. And something moved in that narrow chink – a face maybe, briefly illuminated in the moonlight. Otto had told himself not to get agitated, but now he was getting agitated. He tried to tell himself there was no need. He was the victor here, he had come out on top. There was the van, and in the van was the sofa. There was no need to lose his self-control. He could take it easy, nice and calm, he could be patient ... But then he realised that the agitation actually felt good. It gave him extra power, and it felt right. He had the right to get agitated. He had the right to take revenge.

Otto laughed out loud as he walked to the back door of the van. He laughed and hummed and clenched his billhook, its blade making small, quick cuts in the frozen air. He reached the van just as the chorus began again.

'Eye of the Tiger'.

Otto wrenched the door open, and to his surprise saw the pair who had run him over – the old man and his carer – and he realised two things. It seemed agitation was a bad thing after all. And that his whole life was one huge midden, full of shit and all other kinds of effluent.

Anneli Kukkorinne had backed into the furthest corner of the van's cargo space, which gave her a ringside seat – close enough but far enough away – for what was happening at the van's back door. Just before the doors were flung open, she had heard the music, then the rasping, wolf-like howling laugh, and eventually the heavy footsteps.

And when the doors finally opened and the moonlight flooded inside, lighting up everything, including the new arrival, Anneli watched Erkki move more quickly than she had ever seen him move before. In a single, seamless movement, Erkki dropped down on one knee, his right hand slipped into his jacket pocket, and both hands raised the black pistol and aimed it at the cowboy. After that, two things happened at once: the cowboy stopped laughing and Erkki shot him in the face.

The sound of gunfire wasn't as loud as Anneli had imagined; it sounded more like someone had struck the side of the van with a hammer. A black hole appeared in the cowboy's rugged face, just above the bridge of his nose.

At first, the cowboy looked like he had just received some very bad news. He looked bewildered, perhaps a little disappointed. He stood on the spot, and Erkki, too, appeared frozen in his crouched position. Then, though he had stopped laughing, the cowboy started moving again. His right hand rose, and Anneli saw the billhook, its blade gleaming in the moonlight like a freshly minted silver coin.

Erkki fired again, and another hole appeared in the cowboy's face, this time below his left eye. But this shot too only appeared to have a minimal effect on him. His left eye closed, and he looked like he was suddenly trying to wink at them or scrutinise something carefully. At the same time he looked like he was still trying to move forwards, and his grip on the billhook now seemed firmer than ever.

Erkki must have noticed this too.

He fired again. A hole appeared in the middle of the cowboy's forehead.

This time the cowboy finally started to falter, slowly, as if sinking underwater or into a bed of cottonwool. The billhook fell to the snow. The cowboy stood a moment longer and said in a rasping voice – Anneli wasn't entirely sure, but she could see his lips moving – 'Fuck the lot of you.' He staggered, as though he was deciding whether to topple forwards or backwards, then chose backwards. A cloud of snow puffed into the air, and the cowboy lay on his back in the road.

39

The cab of the truck was warm. The seats were wide and soft, and the vehicle reacted smoothly and precisely to the steering wheel. Ilmari Nieminen felt his arms and legs, and eventually even his fingers, awakening, coming alive again. This, of course, brought his attention to new pains and bruises which, of course, weren't actually new, but it was only now that he noticed them. Nonetheless, he felt better than he had for a long time.

He was sitting high up and looking right ahead; the road was long and straight and, in many places, bathed in bright moonlight. The plan they had hatched had worked, and they would soon be in Kilpisjärvi. That didn't mean that all their problems were now behind them. He had told Antero that the official drop-off point was somewhere between Kilpisjärvi and the Norwegian border, and that apparently they would know when it was time to stop. Antero had considered this for some time, then informed him that he would keep the shotgun within arm's reach, just in case. In light of their recent experiences, Ilmari thought this a sensible idea. Then, a road sign told them they had arrived at Kilpisjärvi.

They passed a few buildings offering tourist accommodation and a large car park, and with that Kilpisjärvi was already behind them. They were alone on the road. The night felt eternal, which, of course, at this time of year it was. The sun wouldn't rise for a few months yet. Ilmari was thinking about his daughter, his ex-wife and the instrument shop in Helsinki, when Antero said he saw something up ahead, on the left-hand side of the road, Ilmari snapped out of his reverie.

Ilmari trained his eyes on the spot of light that grew the nearer they came to it. The road was long, straight as a ruler; they were the only people on it. The spot of light came nearer, and Ilmari soon realised that it was a fire.

The fire was burning in a dark metal can and appeared to indicate the place where a narrower lane turned off the main road, the first of its kind since Kilpisjärvi. Ilmari slowed down, Antero reached for the shotgun and held it in his lap. Ilmari brought the truck to a stop, and they both looked down the lane and saw another burning lantern about a hundred metres ahead. Ilmari and Antero glanced at each other. Antero nodded first, then Ilmari did the same. He put the truck in gear and steered it into the lane, which had recently been ploughed. Ilmari had the impression that it had been ploughed specifically for this purpose. They drove slowly, cautiously, reached the second lantern and looked around at their destination.

The clearing was small and hidden behind a small knoll. On the other side of the clearing was a third lantern with three people standing to its left. Parked behind them was a white Volkswagen Transporter. The line-up looked like it had been carefully planned. At least, that was Ilmari's impression as he approached the group.

The row of people standing waiting for him didn't seem at all fazed at the sight of the truck's front lights. Ilmari drove first towards the Volkswagen, then turned the steering wheel and brought the truck to a halt so that its right-hand flank was facing the line of people. He told Antero it was probably a good idea for him to stay in the cab with the shotgun a moment longer and to watch events unfold. Antero agreed, rolled down his window and cocked the shotgun in readiness.

Ilmari opened his door, hopped out, went round to the back

of the truck and walked right towards the trio. The burning lantern and the moonlight made it easier to see, and Ilmari noticed that the three figures were in fact women of various ages. But it was only once he got up close that he realised they were all wearing nun's habits and headdresses beneath their winter clothes. Ilmari stopped in front of them.

'We were expecting a light-blue van,' said the middle nun.

She spoke English, but Ilmari could hear it wasn't her native language. He quickly glanced over his shoulder. In the glow of the flames, the black Sisu truck looked even blacker than before.

'We ran out of fuel,' he said, aware that it sounded like he was speaking English for the first time since leaving school. 'So, we had to find another vehicle. We exchanged it for this.'

Ilmari knew that what he was saying must sound absurd, but he wanted to be honest. He quickly studied all three women. The nun on the left was considerably older. And she was holding a pistol. This felt at odds with her general appearance, but Ilmari had to admit that he wasn't familiar with the religious practices of all denominations. The right-hand nun was the youngest, and she had the sternest face of the three, as though she had spent her life standing outdoors, and most of it in a bad mood. The one in the middle was around Ilmari's age; her eyes looked careful and intelligent.

'I take it you're expecting this delivery,' he enquired. He had intended it as a question, but his intonation in a foreign language was wrong, and it sounded more like a statement of fact.

'That very much depends on the nature of the delivery,' said the middle nun.

'The finest antique,' said Ilmari. 'And one extra item, about eighty kilos.'

'He's put on weight,' said the eldest nun.

'Sounds about right,' said the middle nun.

The middle nun was about to walk towards the truck when Ilmari raised a hand and stopped her.

'We've been promised a fee for delivering the goods,' he said.

The middle nun looked at the eldest, who gave a nod and looked at the youngest. The youngest nun turned, walked to the back of the Transporter, slid the side door open, took something from inside, then slid the door shut again. She turned and walked right up to Ilmari, then handed him a small black bag bearing the words *Sisters of Mercy*. He had never heard of an order of nuns by that name.

He looked inside the bag and saw an envelope. He glanced behind him. Antero's shotgun was aimed at all of them. Not the best scenario, he thought, but it's better than nothing. Ilmari took the envelope from the bag, opened it. It contained the agreed sum of money. He returned the envelope to the bag, walked over to Antero's window and handed it to him.

Then he walked behind the truck, lowered the hydraulic lift and climbed onto it. First, he pushed the sofa to the edge of the lift, then a little over it, leaving part of it hanging in mid-air. He took out a large plastic tarpaulin and jumped down with this in his hand, then laid the tarpaulin out on the ground. He gripped the sofa's legs, pulled it towards him, and once its centre of gravity had shifted enough, he tilted it onto the tarpaulin.

The procedure wouldn't have pleased a living person, but right now nobody was complaining. The sofa was now lying on its back on the tarpaulin, which, as it was about to be pulled along the ground, was best. Ilmari had some difficulty getting started, but once the tarpaulin finally started moving, he managed to drag it in front of the row of nuns in a matter of minutes. One last burst of energy to lift it upright, and eventually that too was done.

And there it was. The sofa.

It was even grander and more beautiful than when he had first laid eyes on it, he thought. For a moment, nothing happened. Then, the youngest of the nuns approached the sofa carrying a crowbar, and in four sharp movements she had removed the back section. It fell on the tarpaulin. She lifted it out of the way, crouched down behind the sofa and reached her hand deep inside it. About twenty seconds passed. Then the nun stood up.

'It's Dad,' she said quietly.

The other nuns nodded. The middle one helped to reattach the back section where it belonged, then they all gripped the tarpaulin and started dragging it towards the Transporter.

For a fleeting moment, Ilmari felt the urge to ask what this was all about – the sofa, driving it all the way up here, the dead criminal, or father – then he thought better of it. The desire to ask disappeared by itself, dissolved into the trials and tribulations of the journey, the difficulties they had overcome, his own exhaustion. He knew what he knew, and that was enough. He had completed his winter job, even though the weather and conditions had indeed been murder. He turned, walked towards the truck and heard the middle nun's voice behind him.

'Use another vehicle,' she said. 'There's a burgundy Volvo 240 in the car park outside the Kota Motel in Kilpisjärvi. The keys are above the rear, right-hand tyre, inside a lump of snow. The tank's full. Use that.'

Ilmari turned, held the nun's gaze. She seemed to see right into his soul. That's what it felt like.

'Thank you,' he said.

'Thank *you*,' said the middle nun. 'I hope the journey has given you guidance in more than just a geographical sense.'

Ilmari looked at the nun a moment longer. 'That's one way of putting it.'

She nodded. 'The Lord works in ... mysterious ways.'

Ilmari and Antero left the truck at a car park a short distance
from the motel, walked to the motel's own car park and located
the Volvo and the keys. Ilmari sat in the driver's seat, Antero
slipped a tape into the cassette player. *Heroes*. They stopped only
once before Helsinki.

40

Anneli Kukkorinne had been sitting quietly in the front of the Saab 96 for several hours already. She now knew that Erkki had found her pistol but had kept this information to himself and, in doing so, had saved their lives. She also knew that moving the cowboy under the bridge had been a wise move, as was the decision to tow the van behind them for a while before ditching it. In addition, she knew why the fact that it had started to snow again was a good thing: if someone ever found the cowboy, it wouldn't be until much later in the spring.

But there were many other things that Anneli still didn't know, things that bothered her and that, having now regained her ability to speak, she planned to get to the bottom of. The time for questions appeared to have come as Erkki slowed down, turned onto a smaller road and switched off the engine.

'This Saab is probably stolen,' he said, pointing to the bus stop on the main road. 'I think we'd be better off taking the bus.'

Anneli looked at him, his hewn face. his hands that came to an end in thick, stumpy fingers, black from all the engines he had fixed in the last few days.

'It's hard to follow anyone in a bus,' she said.

Erkki kept his eyes on the bus stop, didn't turn his head.

'We're not following anyone anymore,' he said. 'Our mission has been completed.'

He didn't seem to expect an answer. He opened the door, got out of the car. Anneli realised she had no choice. The inside of the Saab was so thick with the smell of smoke and alcohol that the freezing atmosphere outside, which Anneli now drew deep into her lungs, felt like thin, mountain air. In the windless evening, snowflakes fell slowly, one at a time. Erkki had opened the boot, and was lifting out their bags and placing them by the car.

'Is that the Secretary's position too?' she asked. 'That our mission is complete?'

'What else can we do?' asked Erkki, still without looking in her direction. 'The sofa is gone, and I'm in no doubt that that duo have got rid of the truck and vanished for good.'

'I didn't ask that,' said Anneli. 'I asked whether that was the Secretary's position.'

'I believe so,' said Erkki.

'Shouldn't we telephone him to make sure?'

'I'm sure he would say the same.'

Anneli rummaged in her pocket, found what she was looking for, and threw it into the boot right in front of Erkki's eyes. Erkki dropped his bag to the ground, a half-full packet of cigarettes fell out into the snow. He looked at the shiny brochure from the auction house.

'Is this why you're sure?' asked Anneli.

Erkki didn't move.

'You left that in the woods after doing your business,' she said. 'And right from the outset, you've been telling me that the Secretary is the one who takes care of selling the items we acquire and that you don't know anything about how or where they are sold or for how much. But that's not true. You know perfectly well. And when I think of the number of times you've said you'd spoken to the Secretary or he'd spoken to you, but there's no way you could have done, I can only reach one explanation. You *are* the Secretary.'

Erkki didn't move for a long time. Then, very slowly, he stood up straight.

'Or...' he said, still without looking Anneli in the eyes.

'Or what?'

Erkki sighed, a cloud of breath puffed up in front of his face, then dissolved into the snowfall. Now Anneli finally managed to make eye contact with him.

'There is no Secretary,' he said eventually. 'There never was.'

'Excuse me?'

'I'm not in contact with anyone,' he said. 'And nobody gives me orders. I just know some people, and everything else I made up.'

Anneli was sure the ground wasn't shaking at this precise spot on the planet, but the earth under her feet still felt unstable.

'So, who have you been telephoning from all these petrol stations and motels and bars and phone booths, every time you told me you were going to talk to the Secretary?'

'Well,' said Erkki, and by now he sounded decidedly uncomfortable. 'That depended on the situation. Mostly my sister.'

'Your sister?'

'I was telling her what I was up to,' he nodded. 'Not that she was very interested...'

'You've been lying to me,' said Anneli.

Erkki gave another sigh, another small cloud of breath appeared, then disappeared just as quickly.

'I'm sorry about that,' he said. 'It's been bothering me. I tried to make it up to you back then, by shooting that madman. So you wouldn't have to do it. So it wouldn't be on your conscience, if you ever change your mind.'

'Change my mind?' she asked. 'About what?'

'About ... everything,' said Erkki. 'Communism, maybe.'

'What's that supposed to mean?'

'If you ever have second thoughts about it,' he said. 'I've seen it happen.'

'If you ever see something like,' she said, 'you should report it immediately.'

Right away, Anneli realised what she had said. Who would Erkki report it to? His sister? Now it was Anneli's turn to sigh.

'All I'm trying to say,' Erkki continued, 'is that seeing as I took that particular responsibility for myself, you have the possibility to be or not to be whatever you decide in the future.'

Anneli took another deep breath. She heard what Erkki was saying, though it didn't particularly please her.

'Thank you,' she said, 'for thinking about that.'

'You're my friend,' he said.

'Right,' Anneli nodded.

They stood for a moment in silence.

'I just don't...' she began, trying to find the right words. 'I'm not sure I really understand why.'

'Why what?'

'Why we've been doing this,' she said. 'All these years.'

Erkki's eyes were suddenly bright and familiar.

'To build a better world, of course,' he said. 'That's what we're fighting for, right?'

'But if the party doesn't know that we ... If *nobody* knows about what we're doing...'

Now Erkki looked genuinely confused, as though he had heard something unfathomable.

'What does it matter?'

'What...?'

'Exactly,' he said, and to Anneli it looked like he had either suddenly grown in height or otherwise stood taller than he was. 'If you work towards the common good, does it matter whether anybody knows about it?'

Anneli was about to say something but suddenly didn't know what. She watched as Erkki picked up his cigarettes from the snow, put them back in his bag and closed the boot, lifted his and Anneli's bags and walked off towards the bus stop. She felt the snowflakes against her face. She stood on the spot for a long while, then set off after him.

41

Ilmari Nieminen looked at the piano, its shiny black surface and bone-white keys, like an endless row of Hollywood teeth...

But, no ... he wasn't watching the piano; he was watching Helena, her fingers moving across the keyboard, the small movements of her back and shoulders as she seemed to dive and swim with the music. The piece was pretty, just right for Christmas Eve and for home – Helena's home.

Ilmari had got the sheet music from the instrument shop, which he had reached only moments before it closed. He had found the tall composer-cum-salesman again lurking behind one of the pianos with an expression on his face of deep concern – about what, was unclear – and had witnessed his enormous, joyful, tearful relief as Ilmari started counting banknotes onto the counter by the till. The composer-salesman had first tried to hug Ilmari but settled instead for giving him the score of a new piano piece he had just written.

Which Helena was now playing.

Ilmari cautiously looked at Tuulikki. She was sitting on the other side of the living room, right next to the kitchen door. Ilmari caught the smell of the swede gratin and Christmas ham. Tuulikki hadn't asked him to stay, but neither had she asked him to leave. Besides, they hadn't had a detailed conversation about Christmas arrangements or even about whether Tuulikki and Helena were expecting guests. Now Tuulikki looked back at him, and he saw those familiar brown eyes, that familiar smile, which he realised he had missed more than he had allowed himself to admit. He did his best to answer the smile in kind but felt a certain roughness, a tightness in his throat. He nodded and was about to turn away when the telephone rang, and Tuulikki got up to answer it. Ilmari swallowed, with difficulty, then heard Tuulikki's voice:

'It's for you.'

Ilmari walked into the hallway, where the telephone was situated, took the receiver from Tuulikki's hand, caught the subtle scent of her hair, and pressed the phone to his ear.

'Merry Christmas,' said his Aunt Maria. 'I'm so glad I caught you here.'

'And to you,' said Ilmari before he could think of a proper answer.

'Spending Christmas Eve with the family, are you?'

Ilmari looked towards the living room, heard the sound of the piano, smelt the gratin and the ham, and saw Tuulikki walk past the Christmas tree.

'That would be nice,' he said.

His aunt paused for a second or two before answering.

'Helena plays beautifully, doesn't she,' she said.

Ilmari agreed; she certainly did.

'I'm so happy you survived the journey,' said his aunt. 'Both of you.'

Ilmari agreed, again, and reminded his aunt that there was no need to worry about him. He realised something else too. Ilmari hadn't mentioned Antero, yet somehow his aunt knew they were both safe, wherever they were. But before he could say anything, his aunt continued.

'There's someone else here who would like to wish you a merry Christmas.'

Ilmari listened as the receiver was passed from one hand to another and crackled as it was positioned next to the speaker's ear.

'Evening,' said Antero.

'Evening,' said Ilmari.

'Moved the piano by yourself, then?'

Ilmari told him what had happened. He had stopped at the petrol station in Sörnäistenranta, waited a moment, and seeing two men getting out of a vegetable delivery van, he had walked up to them and asked if they could do with a handsome Christmas bonus for an hour's work. They had accepted on the spot.

'After that, plus the price of the piano and the reservation fee,' said Antero, 'you probably don't have a penny left for yourself.'

'That wasn't the point,' said Ilmari.

'Anyway, now you know why I got out of the car halfway back,' said Antero, 'and who I telephoned.'

'Now I know,' said Ilmari, paused, then continued. 'And you kept your promise.'

'It felt important,' said Antero.

Again, Ilmari looked towards the living room. The twinkling of the candles on the Christmas tree seemed to be warming and spreading out, then he realised that it was his own eyes welling.

'It is important,' he said.

Neither man spoke. With one ear, Ilmari heard the electric hiss of the phone, with the other, the piano.

'Have you thought about what we discussed on the drive home?' Antero asked eventually.

'Setting up a delivery firm?'

'Yes,' said Antero. 'Or, to be more specific, a very special delivery firm.'

'Indeed,' said Ilmari. 'As a matter of fact, I have,' he added quickly. 'With certain reservations, as we discussed.'

'We have experience, and we like a challenge,' said Antero. 'But we want to know what it is we're delivering.'

'Exactly.'

'I'll be coming to Helsinki in the New Year,' said Antero. 'Shall we continue planning it then?'

'Sounds good.'

'Merry Christmas, Ilmari.'

'Merry Christmas, Antero.'

His aunt returned to the phone and gushed about a new recipe she had found for a starter of garlic-marinated herrings, which went in one ear and out the other. They wished each other a merry Christmas, and after replacing the handset Ilmari walked back into the living room, stood for a moment listening to Helena's playing, took a few steps towards the kitchen door and saw Tuulikki, half hidden behind a cupboard. Ilmari made sure Helena was still engrossed in her playing and couldn't hear him.

'I'm sorry,' he said. 'For everything.'

He could see that Tuulikki froze, stood perfectly still for a moment, then turned, coming almost completely into view.

'I know,' she said.

'And you know what I was like,' he said.

'Yes,' she said.

'But I think I've learnt something,' said Ilmari. 'These last few days.'

'You sound a bit different,' said Tuulikki. 'As if you really have changed.'

Ilmari didn't say anything at first.

'I don't know what your...' he stammered, 'your situation is, and I don't—'

'My situation?' she asked. 'You mean Lauri?'

'I don't want to—'

'I think you do,' said Tuulikki.

'Right,' Ilmari admitted and felt just as uncomfortable as he had done a while ago.

'How do I know you'll talk to me this time?' she asked, finally stepping out from behind the cupboard door. 'And that you won't keep me at arm's length?'

Ilmari had thought about this on the drive back to Helsinki and still hadn't come up with a better solution than the one that had been staring him in the face all along.

'I promise,' he said.

Tuulikki said nothing. She stepped closer. Ilmari looked her in the eyes. She stopped right in front of him, raised her right hand. Ilmari instinctively replied by raising his own hand. Tuulikki handed him the napkins she had taken from the cupboard.

'Then you can lay the table for Christmas dinner,' she said.

Tuulikki smiled, and Ilmari felt their fingers touch. Just then, he noticed that the piano playing had stopped, and Helena was calling them both into the living room. He was now holding Tuulikki by the hand, and she let him, as they turned and walked towards the beautiful melody.

It was time for a new song.

ACKNOWLEDGEMENTS

The Winter Job was in many ways a great pleasure to write. (Of course, the usual obstacles still remained: the desperation and the doubt that accompany any writing project, the deadlines that always approach at the most inappropriate times, and so forth.) One of the pleasures this time around had to do with the timing of the story, the year 1982. I enjoyed revisiting bits of that era, remembering stuff and looking at photos and pictures, and watching films, and reading articles and books from that particular year and decade. But most of all, I enjoyed listening to the music. And this is where I have to give my biggest thanks. My big brother, Tapio, thank you for the best collection of vinyl known to any eleven-year-old – as I was in 1982 – anywhere. Many of those records found their way into this book.

Additionally, I would like to thank the following people:

Karen Sullivan, the publisher of Orenda Books, works harder than anyone in the book business. I have been very fortunate to work with Karen for over a decade, through book-tour snowstorms to winning awards in balmier weather and generally having a good time.

David Hackston, translator extraordinaire, translated this book from the original Finnish to perfect English. It's far from an easy task, but, as David can perform miracles, here we are – once again.

West Camel edited this English version and did it in his utmost professional, precise manner. My texts have always been in the best of hands with West and I am grateful for that.

Cole, Danielle and everyone else at Orenda Books – thank you for all the hard work. It is much appreciated.

Thank you to booksellers, bloggers, reviewers, booklovers and readers everywhere. Each and every time you talk about books, the good in the world increases.

Finally, thank you, Anu. You are the best. Always.